# CREAM
## -Pied

## KAT ADDAMS

*For the overcomers, the cycle-breakers, and everyone who has fought to rise above. Keep going.*

*"Partly, I like a bad reputation.
But I also want a reputation of being a good person."*

—Joan Jett

# ONE



Crowds gathered at The Steamy Clam every Saturday night since I'd made my debut onstage and twirled around the pole. I had made eight hundred dollars that night, and by the size of the audience tonight, I hoped I could make even more. I wasn't entirely broke, but a string of bad boyfriends had left me in a mountain of debt that I'd been digging my way out of for years. For some reason, I attracted the laziest, trashiest, and brokest douche bags around.

With my time pulled between working two jobs, I barely made it to my new passion, volunteering with disadvantaged youth at the cottage. Those kids had seen and lived some of the darkest moments imaginable. I wasn't a stranger to that life either, so I did my best to help them through that. We would work on art projects, play sports, and do homework or anything else that came up. The most important gift I could give the children was my steady and positive presence in their lives. That was why I had been running myself crazy, working at The Steamy

Clam at night. I planned on quitting after I paid off my debt and devoted more time to do the volunteer work that made me truly happy and fulfilled.

Of course, my life as a dancer had been kept under wraps at the cottage. Not because I was ashamed of my job, but because most people found that depressing as hell. The stigma surrounding strip clubs always included blow and prostitution. But in my experience, it was all about women supporting other women and a judgment-free zone. Still, I couldn't go around, telling children that. The kids at the cottage all knew me as the taco truck lady who had risen above her traumatic childhood and was making it on her own. Of course, I had also left out the fact that I was broker than shit because of my dumbass ex-boyfriends.

At this point in my life, I was finally getting my shit together. I felt a calling to let the youth of the world know that they could rise above the shitty cards they'd been dealt too.

I swiped a bold lipstick across my lips and readied myself in front of the mirror, carefully sticking red heart pasties over my nipples and adjusting my G-string. I shook my fingers through my hair, fluffing it up and out until it looked like I'd stuck my finger in an electric socket. Bigger was always better—with everything.

The last dancer, Kiki, filed in, pulling money from her boots and G-string and winking at me. Kiki had taught me the ropes of the club not long ago. She had been working the pole for six years and helped me nail all of my spins, climbs, and inverted moves.

"Those are the moneymaking tricks," she had told me back when I was fresh meat at the club.

Men loved it when dancers were facedown and ass up, gyrating on the pole. If I could hold myself upside down while booty-popping for twenty seconds, she had told me that I would earn double my usual payout per dance. I'd made a mental note to work on staying up as long as possible and slowing the blood rush to my head. The quicker I was paid, the faster I was gone out of here.

Of course, no one back home in the trailer park I had grown up in would be surprised that foul-mouthed Nikki Vinco had grown up to become Crystal Cream Pie, Outer Fork's most eligible stripper. At least, I didn't have the ten kids and ten different baby daddies that everyone had expected in my future.

I knocked on wood and counted down the days until my period as I left the dressing room and headed toward the stage. Babies wouldn't ever be in my future. I still wasn't even sure if I wanted a husband. My friends with benefits had worked well for me over the last few years, and now that I was twenty-eight, I still didn't feel my biological clock ticking.

I preferred working with older kids. The kids old enough to wipe their butts and blow their noses. I wasn't at a point in my life where anything remotely like having a family was in my future. I had wanted the whole sit-down-around-the-dinner-table family dynamic when I was younger, but after living without it for so long, I had been disillusioned not to care. It was probably all fake anyway. I had seen more than enough wedding rings on the hands of men slipping dollar bills into my panties.

I had no shame, working as Crystal Cream Pie. If I had to get my hands dirty to get where I was supposed to be in life, I would. Besides, stripping was only my side hustle. My full-time job was on board The Pink Taco Truck with my DTF crew. Dirty. Tough. Female. I couldn't think of a better way to describe our girl gang.

My friends had supported me throughout my string of bad men, and I'd done the same for them. We all had stories to tell and drama to air, but luckily, this year, things were beginning to fall into place for all of us. With steady money from the taco truck and my side gig of dancing, my debt grew smaller and smaller, which meant financial independence was quickly becoming within reach—finally.

I sauntered out onto the stage and looked out into the crowd. My palm gripped around the pole, and I let myself fall into it and twirl before wrapping my legs around it and climbing up. The music echoed off the walls, drowning out the men catcalling me from the side of the stage. I winked at them all, blew kisses, and performed a few tricks in the air before crashing down into the splits. I humped my way across the floor in a move called The Snail Trail and made my way toward the guests shaking their money at me. I shoved my boobs in everyone's faces and motorboated my way to a debt-free life.

*This is so easy.*

I pushed myself up to my knees and crawled back to the pole. My gig was almost up, and I needed to flip upside down, so these horny men would lose their control and throw all their money at me. I wrapped my legs around the cold steel and climbed to the top, looking out and into the crowd. A tall man with a lumberjack beard sat, watching me from a dark corner in the back. I had noticed him plenty of times over the last few weeks, but he hadn't yet made his way close enough to the stage to stuff any money in my bra. He stayed in that corner night after night but never once asked me for a lap dance.

I sat at the top of the pole, leaning back onto my hand and spreading my legs as wide as they could go before readying myself to flip over. I stared at the bearded man in the back, locking eyes with him. He reached up to stroke his beard and stared back, eye-fucking me from across the room. I began to slip as my palms and the rest of my body broke out into a sweat. I held on as tight as I could, but it was no use. I couldn't make my inverted moves. I couldn't even hang on. When the song came to a stop, so did I—crashing down and landing so hard on my half-naked ass that the sound of my downfall echoed across the suddenly silent room.

The tall, bearded man stood up, leering at me as if he had an internal conflict on making his next move. His hand clutched his heart underneath a flannel shirt.

Kiki rushed to my side, helping me hobble offstage.

"Are you okay? You didn't hurt anything other than your ego, right?" Layla said after I told her and the rest of DTF about my fall at The Steamy Clam.

"She didn't even hurt that. Don't you know Nikki by now? She doesn't give any fucks. She picked herself up and moved on," Betty said, shaking her head at Layla.

"Well, I would have been mortified! I wouldn't be able to show my face, or my ass, again at that club. Do you think it will hurt your Crystal Cream Pie career?" Layla asked.

"First of all, it's not my career. And most of those men were so drunk, they probably forgot about it before the night ended anyway." I shrugged, hopping out of the taco truck to set up tables.

A line already snaked out into the street, and we weren't set to open for another fifteen minutes.

"You sure you're okay?" Rox said, following behind me.

"Yep. I'll manage. It wasn't that big of a deal," I sighed.

"No. Come here. Look at me." Rox reached out and grabbed my arm.

"Fine. My ego was hurt a little. But just a little. And only because of this guy there." I slumped my shoulders forward.

Typically, men were easy for me to figure out, but my hairy stalker distracted me.

"What man?" Rox asked.

"This lumberjack guy. He is there every night, watching me. I can't figure out if it's creepy or flattering. Anyway, I think his stare made me lose my grip and crash. I don't know. Can't figure it out. He's not my type anyway. I've never really cared for beards, and he was dressed in flannel."

"Beards and flannel, eh? Maybe he was about to go to a hoedown."

"Exactly. Not my type. No business suits, no making it rain on me, no spoiling me like how I deserve. You know I had a man pay me six hundred dollars for a thirty-minute lap dance the other day? That's what I'm looking for—but on a regular basis. Someone who has enough money never to get me in debt."

"And you damn well deserve it. You're worth that and more. Don't settle for another broke loser," Rox said before returning to our task.

I watched her set the tables up as she smiled and hummed, dancing around the parking lot. The hot summer sun shone down on her in a way that lit her up like an angel. Though I knew none of us were angels, Rox would be the closest to anything spiritually positive. She was my hero. This time last year, none of us had been humming, smiling, or laughing. But today, Rox's fresh attitude brought me back to my truth and the task before me of moving up and moving on.

I clasped my palm around the iolite crystal that hung around my neck. When I had read that iolite increased financial well-being, I'd placed the crystal everywhere in my home. I always kept it around my neck as a reminder that I alone could take control of my situation and improve my life—even if that meant rolling around half-naked on a stage.

"Come get your grub on!" Betty shouted out the window, ringing the dinner bell that Layla had recently installed on the truck.

"Shit! I'm not ready yet!" I yelled. I threw the tables and chairs together as quickly as possible, aware of the customers rolling their eyes and tapping their feet around me.

We were parked at the corporate park again today, which meant our customers were typically impatient buttholes—Bluetooth in the ear, no manners, no tips.

DTF had asked me not long ago if I wanted to take charge of our new taco truck that frequented the other side of town, but I politely declined. I didn't want to lose my friends. If I couldn't come to work every day, laughing and being my inappropriate self, then I didn't want to even go into work. Lately, my life had been heading slowly in the direction I was hoping for. I didn't want to jinx myself. Besides, Mercury had been in retrograde when they asked me. That had been a big hell no from me.

"Come on," Rox said, pulling my arm back to the kitchen. "Jay is stopping by for lunch, and I need to work through this crowd, so I can catch a quick break when he gets here." A mischievous grin played across her lips.

"I swear you haven't stopped smiling since divine intervention led you two together. I need that to happen to me. Think a rich, hot sex god will fall out of the sky and save me from making the same mistakes I did with the broke douche bags of my past?" I asked, climbing into the truck.

"Nope. And if he did, you are still going to work your ass off to be an independent woman and not ever depend on a damn man," Betty said, handing me an apron.

"I hate to admit it, but Betty is right. I still have faith you'll find your Prince Charming!" Layla gushed. Her eyes darted off dreamily into the distance.

"Not sure I want a Prince Charming, but I'll take a Lord of the Underworld. We can dress in leather, tie each other up with chains, and perform tantric sex under the full moon. Maybe throw some whiskey shots in there, and that would be my ideal night," I said, nodding my head in agreement with the love life I had planned for my future.

"Good Lord!" Betty shook her head.

"Well, sex under a full moon sounds romantic at least," Layla sighed.

When I returned to The Steamy Clam on Saturday night, after I had literally busted a move during my last performance, I noticed the same bearded man at the same corner table, staring at me with the same intense gaze. I couldn't shake his stare off of me the entire night. When my time to shine came up, I purposely avoided eye contact with him so that, hopefully, I wouldn't slip and fall flat on my face. I tried to check in with my inner soul and figure out what the hell emotions she was feeling, but my inner soul had no answers either.

I finished my routine and headed toward the back to clean the cream off my boobs. I cream-pied my tits at least once every night because, well, that was what the men— and some women—loved. Everyone loved to stick their face in a chest full of whipped cream—everyone but Beard Man. Not once had he come up to the stage. He only enjoyed a free show from the back.

I huffily brushed a towel over myself, cleaning off the sticky residue from my chest—cream, slobber, and I didn't even want to know what else.

"Nikki! Someone wants a lap dance in the private room." Kiki came running backstage, unbuckling her bra and throwing it to the side. She slipped the rest of her clothes off and began to squirm her way into a schoolgirl costume.

"Who is it? A regular?" I asked, hoping it was the man who'd paid me the big bucks not long ago.

I reached for the whip, remembering he liked it when I spanked him. He was married. He deserved to be whipped. He was an easy client.

"No, I don't know this one," she called before scurrying off again.

I checked my reflection in the mirror, making sure I didn't have any hidden cream in my drawers, and made my way back out into the club and toward the back room. Our private room was the sleaziest room imaginable. We even had one of those leg lamps sitting on a corner table next to a leather couch. It had to be leather because whatever was left in this room after a private show would need to be wiped off. Not that I ever went that far with my clients, but some men were known to explode on touch.

Kiki had told me, one time, she'd backed her ass up into a man and bounced so hard that he jizzed all over his pants and her. He left a wet spot on the leather that she had to clean up. She hadn't been happy about that, but at least the man had shamefully tipped her more money than she ever made in one night.

I opened the door to the private room, readying myself to bounce my ass clear up to the ceiling. I had only a few hundred dollars left to pay off on one of my credit cards before I could cut it up and throw it out.

I slipped inside the room and shut the door behind me.

"Marry me," came a gruff voice from the dark.

When my eyes adjusted to the darkness in the room, I saw my bearded stalker, down on one knee and presenting me with a wedding ring—a ridiculously large diamond wedding ring. I held my breath while my mind raced as to how best to approach this creepy situation.

"You can't marry someone you don't know! Get up! What's wrong with you?" I spazzed out, straightening myself up to my full height of six feet. I was hoping, if this man was about to pull out a knife, he would get the point that I could be just as crazy, if not crazier.

The man's lips turned down as he shut the jewelry box and pulled himself to his feet, towering over me. The tip of his beard reached the tip of my head. He stood still, looking down at me without saying a word.

"Hey! Earth to the Green Giant up there!" I yanked his beard.

The man's jaw dropped, and his eyes grew wide as he gasped. "You can't treat Dan like that!" He clutched his chest.

"Well, Dan, who refers to himself in the third person, I can't marry you. Sorry! Now, did you want a dance or what?" I put my hands to my hips and my foot in the air, ready to kick him over and onto the couch so I could get this show on the road.

"You're not marrying Dan. You're marrying me." His brows furrowed as if I had offended him.

"No, I'm not marrying you, Dan!" I huffed. This was getting ridiculous.

"I know you're not! It's me! Weston!" he cried, shaking his head.

"I don't know a Weston! Where is Weston, Dan? Who is me?"

At this point, even I was confused. I looked around the room but didn't notice a Weston or Dan or whoever hiding in a corner.

"I'm Weston!" Weston groaned, shoving the jewelry box in his pocket and taking a seat on the sticky leather couch.

"I thought you were Dan!" I crossed my arms over my chest and stuck my fists in my pits so that I wouldn't punch him in his face. The clock was ticking, and I wasn't getting paid to stand here and argue with his split personality.

"This is Dan!" he said, pointing to his beard.

I blinked. "Your beard?"

"Yes!" He threw his hands in the air.

"Your beard is named Dan?"

"Finally! Bingo! You got it!"

"Are you fucking kidding me?"

"No. Now, will you marry me—Weston!" His voice rose in an octave I'd never heard before on a grown man. Maybe a gremlin, but not a grown man.

"No! I will not marry you, Weston. I also won't marry Dan!" I reached out and flicked his beard, making him gasp again.

"This is just not working. I thought you were the one. I was wrong, I guess." He slumped his shoulders forward and put his head in his hands.

I took a deep breath, realizing I could be dealing with someone a few crayons short of a full box. Empathy kicked in.

*Thanks, inner soul. Where the fuck have you been?*

"Look, you can't propose to someone you don't know. What if we were married and stuck together for the rest of our lives, and I liked the thermostat set at seventy, and you liked it set at eighty-four?"

"That's too hot! I would never!" Weston muttered into his hands.

"Ugh! Point being, I can't commit to someone I don't know, and neither should you! No matter if she is a hot piece of ass who can shake her moneymaker."

"Wait a minute. You want me to commit to you?" He laughed, leaning back onto the couch and spreading his arms to rest against the back cushions.

"Oh my gosh, Weston—Dan—whoever you are, you just asked me to marry you! That's a commitment! Are you on drugs or something? This is insane. I've got to go. I have other clients who would be paying me right now, and that's what I need—money. Not a man groveling at my feet who doesn't even know his real name."

"I'm Weston Banks." He cleared his throat. "I didn't want you to come in here and dance for me. I don't need that. I also didn't want you to *marry me*, marry me."

I sucked in my breath. I had heard that name before. His family owned Westy's amusement park, the diner, a hotel, and pretty much everything else on that side of town. I bit my lip, second-guessing my decision to marry someone who had more money than I'd likely ever see in my lifetime. I glanced at his flannel shirt and scuffed boots. He certainly didn't look the part of wealthy old money.

"That's what marrying means. It's a commitment. You were on one knee. What do you mean, *marry you*, marry you?"

"It's fake. The ring! And the wedding. Or there will be no wedding. I just need you to be my fake fiancée. Only for a little while—until my parents sign over their properties to me instead of my shithole brother, Wes. They are about to retire, and it's been an ongoing feud for over a year. They want to make sure I am carrying on the Banks tradition, and that starts with getting married and having babies."

I pinched the bridge of my nose and plopped myself on the couch next to him. "I know who you are. I thought you took control of the park and hotel and all already."

"No. I wish. Those are rumors. I'm trying to though. I think I can do a better job at it, but don't tell my mama that!"

I sank into the couch.

"Let me get this straight, Weston. You want me to pretend to be your fiancée for a while, so your parents sign over their assets to you instead of your asshat brother, Wes? Which, by the way, what the fuck? Your names are so damn confusing. Anyway, moving on. What do I get out of pretending? You said that ring is fake. So, what's in this for me? Why would I want to put up with the stress and Dan?"

"Because, first of all, Dan's fucking awesome." He stroked his beard. "And secondly, you said you wanted money. I have plenty. That's never been a concern of mine. Rather I didn't have it, to be honest. I don't need it."

*Good. I do.*

"How long do I have to play this charade? And what all does it entail?" I sighed.

"Not long at all. You'll accompany me to my family's big Fourth of July celebration. We make up a good story and set a wedding date—a fake one, relax. And then, boom, you are free once I sign. I'll say you left me."

"What? Why do I have to be the bad guy? Maybe you're a cheating bastard!"

"I would never! We can come up with something. Do you think that would work? Are you willing to get into some harmless shenanigans with me?"

My eyes trailed over his pouty lips tucked inside his bushed-out beard. His eyes could only be described as harmless.

"If you pay me well enough and don't be an asshole, then it's a deal."

I stuck my hand out to shake his hand. His long, bony fingers gently wrapped around my palm. I absentmindedly bit my lip and lowered my eyes to do a bulge check. If his dick size was in tune with his height, maybe I could make another friend with benefits—in the plural, meaning sex and spoiling, even if he was awkward as fuck.

"Deal," he said.

"Why didn't you just lead with the fact that you only wanted me to be your fake fiancée instead of freaking me out like that?" I asked.

"Because you're a hot piece of ass who can shake her moneymaker, and I thought it would be worth a try to have you as mine if you let me." He shrugged.

"Nice try, Dan." I gently ran my palm down his beard before bopping his nose with my fingertip. I pushed myself off the couch and headed toward the door.

"Can I at least still get a lap dance?" he said, reaching out and grabbing my arm before I could get away.

"Really? Ugh! I have a feeling this fake marriage is going to last all of two days. Tomorrow night, Scarlett

Herb on the square. Seven o'clock on the dot to discuss how this is going to go down. Be there or forget it." I shrugged his arm off of mine and left.

# TWO



*Stupid, stupid me*, I chastised myself as I left The Steamy Clam and hoisted myself up into my truck.

I had been driving out here to Outer Forks every chance I got to nail down a woman far enough from home to not raise suspicions, but close enough to bring around my parents now and then for show-and-tell.

So far, I'd only shown them my failed relationships, which they took as an indicator of my business sense. That didn't make sense either. I could balance books, bring fresh ideas to the table, run a ship with the right crew, and be the boss man that all of the honies loved. But still, that wasn't good enough for my parents. My ma wanted grandbabies, and my dad wanted tradition. Which meant, Wes and I were competing to see who could wed and bed a woman before the other.

Luckily for me, I was a damn near seven-foot-tall cold drink of water. Wes, on the other hand, was a five-and-a-half-foot tall glass of tea—not sweet tea either, but the nasty real stuff. Bitter and the crap that no one wanted. I started my engine and revved my exhaust, sending vibrating roars throughout the parking lot. Natural habit. Girls loved that shit.

"Weston, you have a date tomorrow with the hot stripper, Crystal Cream Pie. A fake date. For a fake marriage. That, let's just be honest, you want for real because she is hot as fuck," I told myself on the drive home.

I spoke to myself out loud, reasoning the pros and cons of dating a stripper. I didn't have much of a con list. I wasn't a jealous man or possessive. I didn't need to worry about money. I had plenty of that. Marrying Crystal Cream Pie would be fine by me, especially after my past failed relationships.

The last time I'd really liked a woman was Mardi Hall, the lizard lady from our annual sideshow at Westy's. She wasn't really a lizard, but her tongue was forked and stretched up and out past her forehead.

I thought to myself, *Damn, the things she could do with that tongue,* before realizing it was fake.

By the time Lizard Lady showed me her real tongue, which was nothing but a nub in her mouth, I was already head over tails for her. I watched all of her shows and was her biggest fan. But one closer look at that flap of jelly in her mouth had had me running for the hills.

*"It's fake, Weston. Don't you know that?" She held the prosthetic tongue in her hand, shaking it in my face.*

*"Ah! What in the world?" I screamed like a bitch, cringing and stepping back from her slimy appendage hanging in the air.*

*"Oh, come on. Look. It rolls up in my mouth. Watch how it works."*

*She shoved the pink snake into her mouth, but I'd already peaced out.*

I'd avoided Westy's for the rest of the time her show was in town.

Then, shortly after Mardi, I had fallen for another lady named Trina. She was much more stable—or at least her tongue was. She had four children, worked at Nutter—our diner—and could bake a chocolate chess pie that even my ma liked. But there was a problem with our relationship too. Trina wanted me to get rid of Dan. The day she asked me to shave my best-friend beard, I recoiled in horror. I never asked her to get rid of any of her kids, and it was kind of the same thing. My boy Dan was staying. Trina had had to go.

My thoughts bounced back to Crystal.

I had watched her dance several times. I counted her fingers and toes, making sure they were all there. I watched how she handled dire situations, like that time she had fallen on her ass. Not going to lie, that gutted me. I thought for sure she had busted that pretty little tail of hers. But the way she picked herself up again without giving a rat's ass, that was what had done me in.

I liked that attitude of hers. It was the attitude that I needed to take back home and confront my ma because I was too pussy enough to do it.

I drove the rest of my long drive back home with the radio blaring my absolute favorite country tunes as I sang on and on about flannel shirts, jean skirts, and souped-up trucks. That was living the life. I lived in between Westworld, as my family liked to call it, and Outer Forks. Westworld was much closer to the big city, and Outer Forks was much closer to nothing. But that was what I liked—the nothingness of it all. I wasn't a hustle-and-bustle type man. Driving the distance out here wasn't a big deal to me. Sometimes, I would check into a nearby hotel, but I needed to head home tonight and ready myself for my big fake date tomorrow.

I'd never heard of Scarlett Herb, but it sounded like something I would name a tea shop—and I did not like tea unless it was sweet and thick as syrup. I couldn't hold my pinkie out and sip out of a teacup either. I'd tried, but my clumsiness turned much of everything into a disaster. Like that one time I had slipped on a banana peel. I thought that stuff only happened in the movies, but nope. It legit happened to me, of course. As embarrassing as it had been, I'd somersaulted into the air like an Olympian gymnast. That was pretty cool.

I turned into my winding gravel drive, singing loud karaoke to my audience of one—myself. Tomorrow, I was going to win over Crystal. She would be my fake fiancée, but maybe she would give up the goods too. I hadn't had sex since Trina, and that was forever ago. If I could rock Crystal's body in bed, perhaps I wouldn't need to convince my parents of anything. Maybe she really would like me enough to go along with my plan, and then—*bada bing, bada boom*—Westworld would be mine.

I sat at the white-tableclothed booth, sipping a cocktail and waiting on my fiancée. The table I had chosen looked out over the dining hall, which was packed with laughing customers. I watched one man reach over and pat his lady's hand. I watched another woman scoot her chair closer to a man and pinch his butt. I brought my drink to my lips and sighed. I wanted to be touched.

"Well, well, well. Look who we have here. The famous Weston Banks did show up," Crystal said, popping out from the side of the nearly enclosed private dining booth.

"Did you come in from the back door or something? I've been watching for you." I nodded my head toward the entrance.

"Something like that. I know the owners and do some work here, making that right there." She pointed at my drink.

"You bartend?"

"No. I make the Shizzle Sauce ice cube floating in your drink." She slid into the booth.

My eyes immediately shot to her tits, which bounced in her low-cut dress as she wiggled herself into a comfortable position.

"So, you're not just Crystal Cream Pie? You do other stuff too?"

"I'm not even Crystal Cream Pie! The name's Nikki. I am not only a stripper. I work The Pink Taco Truck too."

"The wha—" I shook my head, unsure of if she was offering up sex already.

"The Taco Truck. That's what it was called. But it's pink. So, everyone in Outer Forks knows us now as The Pink Taco Truck. I take it, you haven't tasted any of our food."

"No, not yet. But tacos sound good to me. Speaking of tacos, I'm starving. Do you know what you're getting? I'm assuming you already have some idea since you know the place." I waved my menu, thumbing through it like I didn't know what I wanted. I knew what I wanted. Meat. Steak. Anything, except vegetables.

Our waiter came by, interrupting our conversation and drawing my attention to him instead of Nikki's boobs.

"Oh! Hi, Jesse! I didn't know you were working tonight." Nikki's tone, posture, and mood suddenly changed. Her back straightened up, her chest stuck out, her eyes twinkled, and she purred. Purred!

"Pleasure to see you again, Nikki. Can I get you the usual cocktail?" Jesse grinned, his eyes also locked on her boobs.

"The pleasure is mine, and of course, I'll take the usual. You know me so well." Nikki winked.

I cleared my throat.

"Could we start with some type of meat tray? Something with meat and cheese or anything of that sort?" I asked, breaking the sexual tension lurking between Nikki and Jesse.

"I'm vegan!" Nikki gasped.

"Oh! I'm so sorry. What do they eat? I'll get you whatever you'd like!" I squeezed my hand into a fist, ready to knock myself out. Already, I'd gotten off on the wrong foot.

"I'm just fucking with you, Weston. I'll take the charcuterie too," she said to Jesse, who reluctantly left our table to put in the order.

I had no idea what charcuterie was, but it sounded like a dirty word, and I liked it. Maybe I would get lucky tonight.

"Okay, let's talk business. What are you paying me, and what do I need to do? Also, I'm not a whore, so if you think I'm fucking you for money, you're mistaken. Let me know, as we will end this right here, right now."

"No, not at all," I blubbered, taking a long sip of my cocktail.

*Damn it.*

"Good." She unfolded her napkin on her lap, smoothing it out and leaning back into the booth. "Let's hear it."

"We have a celebration coming up. It's for Independence Day. My family always goes all out with a big party. I thought that would be the perfect time to introduce you—my fiancée—to my family. My dad's looking to retire soon, and he's been commenting on passing down the family business. I want it to go to me. It has to go to me. Wes would run it into the ground."

"So, you need me for just a weekend?" She tilted her head to the side and tapped her chin.

"It's a three-day weekend, and no, that's not all." I sucked in my breath. I hoped I wasn't pushing it. "I need you for six weeks. Whatever it takes. My ma and dad are nosy Nellies. After you meet them, we might be doing dinners or such together to keep up the illusion. I don't know yet. If it drags on before I sign, then maybe longer. I'll pay you a substantial amount." I rubbed my hands together, leaned forward, and threw a number out—a really high number.

Her eyes bulged, but she tried to remain composed. I was a businessman and knew enough about selling to see that I'd sold her.

"Plus, twenty percent travel charge for your weekend away." She narrowed her eyes. "And I'll need a few things for travel, so a stipend of, say … an extra twelve hundred."

"Done."

The waiter brought out our charcuterie plate and Nikki's cocktail, once again ogling her boobs.

"Do you know what you'd like to order?" Jesse asked.

"I'll take the lobster, Jesse. Thanks!" She handed him her menu and licked her lips.

I blew a breath out of my nose, stifling a laugh.

"Best cut of steak you have, over medium for me, please. And potatoes. Any type. Thank you," I said, handing him my menu, too, and turning my attention back toward my fiancée.

"What was that *hmmph* for?" she asked when Jesse left. "Does my ordering lobster bother you?" Her fingers tapped against the table in an impatient rhythm.

"No. I know what lobster means! I didn't know you'd be that easy."

"Easy? Excuse me? What the hell does that mean? What does lobster mean to you? Is this Dan talking again?" She leaned forward, and I swore I saw every single hair of hers bristle.

"Lobster is code word for sex. Everyone knows that! The girl orders lobster when she wants sex. It's like a transaction. Duh!" I laughed.

Her posture prickled even more.

*Uh-oh. This is not that kind of transaction. Retreat. Retreat.*

"If I want sex from you, I'll tell you I want to fuck you. I won't say *lobster.* Now, shake on this business deal before I change my damn mind," she said, her shoulders still raised to her ears, making her look almost as tall as me. Almost.

I stuck my hand out and shook hers, afraid to utter another word until Jesse arrived shortly after with our entrees.

I struggled to be smooth with the ladies. I tried my damnedest to be Rico Suave in life, but I fell flat on my face every damn time. I thought I knew what women wanted, but I was usually wrong. The one consistency in my life and relationships was money. At least I knew Nikki wanted my money.

I swirled my drink in my hand, clinking the cube against the glass and accidentally sloshing alcohol over the top.

"Are you nervous?" she asked between mouthfuls of lobster—not code-word-for-sex lobster.

"Yes."

"About?"

"You. You make me nervous."

"How come? Was it the way I pulled Dan last night? I'm sorry. I'm not a physical person. I was teasing you."

I reached up to stroke my beard, patting him to make sure he was okay.

"You're beautiful and way out of my league. That's why I'm nervous. Every time I saw you up there onstage, I wanted to ask you out. I knew you were the one I wanted to bring home. I saw you smile at all the other men, and you always seemed to treat everyone nice. Your head is always held high. Even when you busted your ass that one time. You seemed like a good fit. It took me several trips to The Steamy Clam to work up the nerve to propose to you. Even if it was fake." I shrugged, busying myself with my steak and not meeting her eyes, which I felt were staring a hole through my soul.

"I noticed you at the club when I worked. I wondered about your story and why a man like you would be there."

"A man like me?" I gently set my fork down but ended up clinking it against my plate loud enough to startle both of us.

"Yes … a man like you. You and Dan are good-looking. Way too good-looking to be hanging out at The Steamy Clam. I think you're a good catch. Just got to watch putting your foot in your mouth. At least with me. And don't ever say anyone is out of your league. There is no league. We are all here on this earth with our feet on the ground. We're the same. Equal footing." She smiled at me. Smiled!

"Thank you. Dan and I are honored."

She laughed and shook her head, grabbing the napkin from her lap and setting it on the table as if she were throwing in the towel.

"So, tell me about Dan. Do you have to oil that thing up? With beard oil or anything?" she asked, taking a sip of her cocktail and leaning back into the booth, watching Dan and me.

"Beard oil? You mean, pussy juice?" I asked without missing a beat.

The silence that fell on the table was deafening. I had done it again—foot in mouth.

*Fuck!*

Nikki stared me down for what felt like an eternity before she roared with laughter. I made her laugh so hard that she started to form tears in the corners of her eyes.

I grinned, giving myself a mental pat on the back.

For the rest of the evening, we grew into a much more comfortable and playful mood. Even Jesse, who had stopped by one too many times, seemed annoyed that Nikki was having a good time with me. I was shocked that she seemed to be having a good time with me too.

We talked over the details of how we would tell everyone we'd met and agreed not to mention her stripper gig. Our plans were easy enough to remember, as they didn't venture much off from her real life. She worked a food truck, and we'd met one day when I had business in Outer Forks. I rarely had business in Outer Forks, but since I worked with marketing all Westworld had to offer, my parents never really checked on what I was up to. As long as I was bringing in the customers, they didn't care.

"Do I get to go to Westy's and jump to the front of the line since I know the owner now?" she asked, guzzling water to sober up before they kicked us out.

Already, the restaurant had slowed, and only a few diners remained.

"If you want. I can even give you a behind-the-scenes tour! Set you up in our hotel for the evening too. I'll throw that in our package deal."

"What are you going to do when your ma and dad find out we aren't together anymore? How will that change things?"

"Maybe I'll have a real girlfriend lined up at that point." I shrugged.

She reached across the table and squeezed my hand. "I'm sure you will." She winked at me.

*Winked! Take that, Jesse.*

# THREE

*Nikki*

I had only a week left before my big debut as the soon-to-be new member of the Banks family. I had left Scarlett Herb after our business meeting with enough cash in my pocket to buy a whole new wardrobe and pay a large sum on one of my last remaining credit cards. I cursed my ex-shithead-boyfriends who'd leeched off of me years ago. Back then, when I had been in those toxic types of relationships, I hadn't thought about my future. I had let them sit on their asses, vaping their douche whistles and playing video games while I slaved as a waitress.

Unfortunately, waitressing hadn't paid the bills, hence the credit card debt. My exes had wanted to use my cards for everything from the latest gaming console to a six-pack of cheap-ass beer, and my dumbass had let them. It wasn't until I met Betty and Rox that I woke up from that vicious cycle. They finally knocked some sense into me and helped me get on my feet by working with them aboard the taco truck. They had taken me under their wings in no time.

Shortly after they'd hired me, Layla had come along in a similar boat, minus the debt.

I had grown with DTF, and they had grown with me. We supported one another and motivated each other to rise above the shitty cards life had dealt us. Last week, I had been an exhausted stripper, and now, here I was, shopping for a new wardrobe and crawling off of a mountain of debt, thanks to my super-rich, new, fake fiancé, Weston. Weston was awkward as hell but kind enough for me to look past his oddball behavior and play into his little game.

That would be all it was for me—just a game. I had enough friends with benefits to call whoever I was in the mood for these days. I didn't need to add to that long list. But I would be lying if I told myself I hadn't had fun with him at the restaurant. He had made me laugh in his own quirky way. He had even made DTF laugh when I recounted our night back to them.

*"So, let me get this straight. He has a beard named Dan, which he lubes with pussy juice instead of beard oil? I don't know if I should be cringing right now or if I should be turned on. I'm a little of both,"* Betty said as we stood, huddled in the truck kitchen during food prep.

*"I've never been with a man with a beard before! Doesn't it get all scratchy between your legs and on your face?"* Layla asked.

*"It's a good kind of pain. Besides, you've always wanted your own divine intervention, Nikki. Maybe Weston is it. He's rich. That's what you said you wanted in a man."* Rox raised her eyebrows.

*"I know; I know. It's just … well … he's different. Weird. A goofball. I did bring up the divine intervention and told him just a little about you and Jay. Nothing too personal. I did get all swoony when I told him Jay called you Kintsugi. And do you know what this big, giant buffoon said to me? He called me a geode. A fucking geode. He said it was because I was tough on the outside but filled with*

*diamonds on the inside. So, you got Kintsugi, and I'm a damn boring-ass rock." I laughed.*

*"That is the sweetest thing! You are a crystal, Crystal!" Layla clasped her hands together and hopped back on her heels.*

*"A rock. That's pretty damn funny! I get what he was trying to say, but—" Betty started.*

*"But a goofball," I said, cutting Betty off. "He's a goofball. Although he is a good-looking goofball."*

*I sighed, checking in with myself to see what my big deal was and coming up with no answers. My only current goal was to pay off my debts. If I had to use the Jolly Green Giant to help me get there, I would be okay.*

*"You're all right. I'll put my best effort into being the best fake fiancée for him. After all, if the universe hadn't wanted this, it wouldn't have put him in my path, in front of my pole." I laughed.*

*"Bet you don't go two days into that trip without being in front of his pole," Betty chimed in.*

*The other girls laughed, but I gasped, putting my hand to my mouth and pretending as if I were offended. I was not. Betty was probably right. Unless Weston continued to put his foot in his mouth so much, he wouldn't be a hard pass for me. I could have a little fun with my soon-to-be fake hubby while also getting paid, too, as long as we both knew this was all an illusion.*

I picked out a few pieces of stylish clothes for myself and a few pieces of more modest attire to wear for Weston's parents. Not only did I need to convince them that I loved their son, but I also needed to convince them that I was a good girl. I was not. But Weston had told me his parents needed to see him with someone stable, family-oriented, traditional, and motherly—all things I knew nothing about.

I hadn't grown up in a family-oriented home, nor were we traditional. My father had left when I was two, and my mother certainly hadn't been *motherly*. She'd had a different boyfriend every other month, and they, too, had blown through her money. Funny how that worked out. Cycles.

The world continued through one long cycle. I'd smashed that cycle through DTF.

*Fuck that.* I patted the cash in my pocket.

The clarity I had in life now was mostly from damn hard work but also the support of my friends, and dare I say, crystals, smudge sticks, chants, and maybe even a naked dance or twelve under the full moon. DTF had gone along with it. All, except Betty, who had made the sign of the cross when I whipped out anything too outlandish, like my Ouija board. Even though she had told us that her African ancestors had participated in voodoo, she wouldn't let anything that crazy into her life.

She had refused to participate and be in the same room with the Ouija board and us that night. When the rest of the DTF clan began to play, I purposely freaked Betty out by making the board spell out her name along with *herpes*. I read every letter aloud, knowing she was eavesdropping. She had gotten pissed and strolled right out of that room, offering to show us her Choco Taco to prove the Ouija board was full of shit.

I gathered my shopping bags and stuffed them in the trunk of my car. I only needed to find a pair of not-so-sexy pajamas to pack, and I would be good to go. Weston had mentioned his mom was traditional—as in, I needed to act like a virgin. No booty shorts and bralettes for bed. I was on the mission for a muumuu before I finished packing. A faint vibration came from my purse as I rummaged through a pile of receipts to find my phone. Weston's name flashed across the screen, making me groan.

"What's up, Weston?" I asked.

"I was making sure we had everything good to go for Friday morning. Are you okay to take time off of work?" he asked.

"Yep. Everything is good. I'm finishing up my shopping now. Just need some un-sexy virgin-style pajamas since you want me to convince your mom I'm some kind of angel." I settled into my seat and started the car. The rock-and-roll music I had been listening to blared through the speakers. I reached for the volume control and turned it down.

"I would have pegged you for more of a polka lover," Weston muttered.

"Really?" I strapped myself in, gripped the steering wheel, and impatiently tapped my thumb.

"I'm kidding. Anyway, it's nice to hear your voice. I've got your pajamas under control. I think we can even wear matching ones. That might seal the deal. I'll pick some up this weekend. Anything else I can do for my fiancée?"

I cringed. "Nope. I think that's it. You're picking me up, right? Are you sure you want to drive out here and then back? That doesn't even make sense."

"I have business out there this week. I'll be staying in a hotel. Besides, I'm chivalrous, my little geode. I'm going to pick my soon-to-be wife up properly."

I cringed again. "Perfect. See you Friday morning. I'll text you the address."

"Laters, baby." Weston clicked his tongue. I was pretty sure he was giving me finger guns that I obviously couldn't see.

I rolled my eyes and hung up the phone. If I could stick this awkward situation out, I would be able to pay off one of my lower-balanced credit cards—the entire credit card. That thought alone excited me enough to put up with Weston and Dan and whatever family drama he could throw at me. If I could handle the shit situation I had grown up in, I could handle him and his overbearing parents.

I turned the volume back up on my radio and rocked out all the way home.

Business had kept me busy throughout the week. I blinked, and Thirsty Thursday at the square was already here, which meant tonight would be packed. With daylight lasting well after eight o'clock these evenings, people bustled along the square in search of good food and good tunes.

If we weren't at the square these days, we parked at one of the many festivals going on in Outer Forks. During the summer months, there were several festivals—music, art, crafts, Renaissance, and plenty of food ones. Both of the taco trucks stayed busy during the warmer months, but even in the winter, we had continually increased profits.

Earl, our founding father—or as I liked to call him, our taco pimp—had even mentioned opening a storefront. Both Betty and Rox weren't thrilled about that. They worried if we became too big, quality control would tank, and our products would suck. With our unique Instagram-worthy Shizzle Sauce collaboration with Scarlett Herb, our social media following had doubled, and so had theirs. People liked us now, but we didn't want to get a big head about it.

I stepped out of the back of the truck to take a quick breather from the constant orders coming in tonight. I leaned my tired back against Rosie, our T. rex mascot painted on the side of the taco truck. I put my palms to my eyes and rubbed, smearing what little eye makeup was left on me after this tiresome day.

"You okay?" Layla poked her head out the back door.

"Yeah. Yes. Just tired. I'll be right in," I answered.

A loud, thumping noise rang out over the bustling square. I turned my head toward where it had come from, noticing a huge, old-school purple car making its way toward me. As it got closer to me, the front of the car reared up and then back down, right in tune with the bass line pounding through its speakers.

I sat, mesmerized, as the hoop-ride car bounced its way right up to me and stopped. Weston stuck his head out the driver's window and winked.

*Fuck.*

"Sweet ride," I said, walking up to his car and admiring the golden interior. "What are you doing here?"

"You like it? It's my pussy wagon. And someone told me something about pink tacos. So, I thought I'd come to try out a pink taco in the pussy wagon." He grinned.

"Pussy wagon!" I bit my lip. I never knew I had a thing for pimp mobiles, but my panties were feeling pretty damn warm at the moment. "And I mentioned tacos. Not pink tacos. It's The Pink Taco Truck."

"Damn it! Thought I was going to get some beard oil for my boy Dan here." He gently patted his beard. "No worries. I'll still try your taco. Let me park the P-wagon."

I shook my head and sighed. If Weston was here, that meant I had to introduce him to DTF. I whispered a quick prayer to the goddesses of shame and hopped back inside the truck. There were only two customers left in line when I got back to work.

"He's here. Weston is here." I blew out my breath.

"What?" Betty asked.

"Nuh-uh!" Layla held her hand to her mouth.

Rox smiled.

"We get to meet your fake husband-to-be?" Layla squealed.

"And Dan?" Betty grinned.

"Simmer down, bitches! I'm already nervous as fuck, and I have no idea why."

I wrestled with the confusing thoughts in my head surrounding Weston, Dan, the P-wagon, and my fake engagement while shushing DTF, who were all doubled over in laughter. I threw my hands in the air, giving up on my so-called friends, and stepped up to the window right as Weston came into view.

"Weston." I smiled. "Welcome to The Pink Taco Truck. These are my friends," I said, making the introductions while simultaneously swatting my hand behind me to let them know to shape up.

"Pleasure to meet you, ladies. I've heard so much about you all and your tacos. Nikki mentioned something about some Shizzle Sauce to me, and I've not been able to get my mind off of it since. So, I thought I'd try it tonight while I'm here." Weston cocked his head to the side, peering at all of us. He was so tall that he could see everything through the window, including my fidgety hands.

I looked behind me at my friends, who were all smiling back at him.

"Don't you worry, baby. I'm going to fix you right up. Go on over there and have a seat at the table. I'm going to bring you the shiz." Betty winked.

"Looking forward to it." Weston turned to walk to a nearby table and sat down.

"Oh my gosh! He is hot! What the hell is wrong with you?" Layla pinched my butt.

"You think so? I've not made my mind up on him yet. He's attractive, but the beard throws me. I've never been with a man with one before," I replied, grabbing a cup full of sweet tea.

"Yes. He is hot! And he seems like the Jolly Green Giant. I don't think he would be the type to be an asshole. But you never know. I say you put feelers out this weekend, and if he is as big of a sweetie pie as he comes off, then hop on Dan and go for a ride," Rox said. She watched Weston as he sat at the table, karate-chopping a fly hovering around his face.

Betty was as busy as ever, making the fanciest plate of tacos I had ever seen. She artfully arranged the cilantro over the top, stepped back, and quietly admired her masterpiece.

"Spill it, Betty. What's wrong? You're quiet. I've never known you to be quiet." I nudged her side.

"All those crystals, spells, and whatever else magic you are always doing, and you can't even see it. That is your man right there. That big, sexy buffoon is that divine intervention mess you are always preaching. He's sexy, he's nice, he's rich. You need some sort of crystal for clarity. He's your one. I don't need no damn Ouija board to tell me that. Watch me work my magic, and when you are married to him and rich as fuck, thank me then. I'll take cash. You're welcome. Now, get yo' butt out there and talk to that man." Betty handed me the plate heaped high with tacos and decorated with dots of Shizzle Sauce.

My eyebrows shot up into my hairline. "We'll see."

I left the truck, balancing the massive plate, napkins, and sweet tea in my hands. "Voilà!" I said, setting Weston's meal in front of him.

"Wow! This looks delicious! Thank you." He beamed, giving me an uneasy feeling in my stomach.

I cleared my throat. "So, about tomorrow. Are we taking the pussy wagon? Do I get to bounce around in that thing?"

"You sure do. I got her all cleaned up and ready to go. We'll be arriving at the farm in style."

"Farm? Like a real farm?"

"Kind of. My ma likes animals, so my dad bought her a cow and some chickens that run around. We also have a pretty big garden. So, if you can call that a farm, then it is. Ma would like more, but business keeps them too busy for her to worry about it much. They have a lot of help, but it never seems to be enough. With them getting up there in age, they can't manage too much more manual labor." He took a bite of his taco, and his eyes rolled in the back of his head. "Goodness gracious, woman! This is a burst of happiness wrapped in a tortilla. And the Shizzle! Smoky, sweet, with a bite. Like you," he continued.

"Glad you know me so well. I'll also set your ass on fire. You'll find that out later. Both from me and the tacos." My voice fell flat as he stopped chewing and pulled his brows together as if he couldn't think and chew at the same time.

"Worth it." He shrugged, finishing his taco and starting on another.

My back was facing the taco truck, but I could feel DTF's eyes on me. I knew what they were doing in there. They were doing the same thing I would be doing if I wasn't sitting out here with Weston.

DTF had this little game where, when it was slow, we would come up with conversations people were having outside the truck. We would all go back and forth, laughing our way through ridiculous scenarios as we made up stories about the people around us. Usually, the stories consisted of vibrators, douche bags, being a ho, or constipation. We had no shame, but we probably should. I could only imagine the sex talk inside the taco truck right now.

I quickly turned my head, looking back into the truck. Sure enough, they all stood, laughing and waving back at me.

"Let me guess. Your friends are watching us," he said, drawing my attention back to him.

"Yep."

"Want to give them something to talk about?"

"What do you have in mind?" I leaned forward. This could get good.

"You can sit on my lap, stroke my beard, profess your love for me." He pushed his plate aside and patted his lap.

"Or you could sit on my lap, stroke my hair, and profess your love for me," I shot back, ready to get into shenanigans.

"I'll crush you!" Weston gasped.

"You've seen my thighs. Do you have any idea how strong they have to be to grip that pole and let me hang upside down? They are made of steel. Hop on." I patted my lap.

Weston rose from the table and walked over to me, squatting down and squishing my legs. I cringed, willing the chair to hold us.

"My beautiful Crystal Cream Pie," he said, stroking my hair and looking into my eyes. "Am I doing it right?" he muttered, not moving his lips.

"Grander. Make bigger gestures." I huffed out, barely able to breathe with a giant on top of me.

He cradled my face with his palm and smoothed his thumb over my lips before leaning down and kissing me. His beard felt surprisingly soft against my face. I closed my eyes, reached behind his head, and pressed his mouth into mine harder.

"This is quite the show," he murmured, still attached to my mouth.

I stuck my tongue in his mouth, taking it even further. He moaned and relaxed his gigantic self on top of me. My nipples hardened under my work shirt.

"Phew!" I said, pulling back. "I think that did it. They're surely mind-blown now. Look at the time!" I checked my watch.

Weston blinked, his lips still parted from our kiss.

"You okay there, big guy?" I tapped Dan.

"Sorry. Yes." He shook his head. "Late. Time. Right. I'll just … I'll …" He stood up. His pants stuck out about a foot, almost knocking me in the face when he turned around.

"Damn. Well, if our make-out session didn't do it, that tent you're pitching in your pants will!" I adjusted myself in the chair.

I needed to sit on my hands to keep from reaching out and curling my fingers around the full thickness of him. His bulge was like nothing I'd seen before.

"Shit!" he said, looking down and covering his dick with his hands. "Couldn't help it! Sorry." He fished his wallet out of his pocket. "Here, put it in the tip jar. Thanks, Nikki. For the tacos and the hard-on. Now, if you'll excuse me, I have to run to the P-wagon before my balls burst." He threw two hundred-dollar bills on the table and ran off.

"Tomorrow at eight, right?" I called out after him.

"Eight!" he answered, jogging to his car.

I gave a wink and a wave at DTF, who stood glued to the windows of the taco truck.

# FOUR

Weston

I rolled out of bed at six a.m. sharp, so I could have ample time to get myself looking hot for my fake engagement getaway to the farm.

Yesterday, when Nikki had stuck her tongue down my throat, I had known then and there that this fake engagement needed to at least get me another one of her sloppy kisses—or more.

I showered, soaping up my balls and butt. Not that I was expecting anyone near my balls or butt, but if the opportunity showed itself, I needed to be a clean, lean string bean. I took my razor out of my bag and stretched my ball sack tight, ready to shave myself smoother than a fish's belly. If I didn't shave, she might get lost in there. Again, not that I was expecting her to be in that general vicinity. But still, if the opportunity showed itself, yada yada.

My burly bear hair was one of two things I was self-conscious about. My ability to grow Dan was also my ability to grow little Dan—as in the 'fro down below. The other was my à la natural penis. I'd once looked up circumcision online and sent Ma flowers, thanking her for not doing that to me. I could live with a dick that looked different than most of my American brothers. It sure beat the alternative.

I hummed to myself, getting a little too carried away with the razor. Before I knew it, I'd shaved my entire nether regions and even my ass. I hoisted one of my long legs up to the soap holder and squatted down into a spread-eagle stance, reaching back behind my balls and making sure I'd rid myself of every gnarly hair attached to me.

"Damn, my dick looks bigger!" I huffed to myself, toweling off.

That whole shaving process had taken the wind out of me. I caught my breath before stretching my legs out and slipping on the sexiest, sleek pair of boxer briefs I owned.

"Weston, my man, time to win over the lady and the parents and get your name on the goods," I told my reflection in the mirror as I pointed finger guns at myself and clicked my tongue.

I ironed my khakis and polo shirt, slipped on my leather shoes, and gathered my things. I had about thirty minutes left before I could see my fiancée, and that was enough time to pick her up breakfast. I hurried out the door, packed my P-wagon, and set about finding a coffee shop in Outer Forks.

With the windows down, I let the fresh morning air blow through Dan. The sun was shining, the weather was perfect, and I couldn't have asked for a better holiday weekend. I tapped my thumb against the steering wheel as I fantasized about all the way things could go right this weekend. I didn't think of how they could go wrong. I refused. I didn't like to put trash into my head. If a situation arose, I'd deal with it then.

I pulled up to the nearest coffee shop and placed an order in the drive-through. I had no idea what Nikki liked—except lobster, tacos, and booze—so I ordered half the menu. She would at least have options. There wasn't any sense in me striking out as soon as our rendezvous began. I loaded the backseat with eight greasy bags of food and crossed my fingers that, with my mouth full, I couldn't put my foot in it at least.

I typed in her address on my GPS and took a long, slow sip of my hot chocolate. Coffee was disgusting. In the morning, I either had a warm glass of milk or hot chocolate with my biscuits and gravy. Growing up at the farm would have buttered me up into a butterball had I not been so damn tall. Lucky for me, I only grew up and not out, so I had no problem indulging in shitty foods.

I followed my GPS's voice to an apartment building not too far from the hotel where I stayed. She had texted me her address last night and told me to pull up right in front of apartment 352A, and she would be right out. She had said that she kept her blinds open, letting in the natural light and meditating in the morning, so she would see me as soon as I arrived.

I ducked my head, looking out over the passenger window and reading the apartment numbers as I passed by. Finally, I found her tucked in the corner of a cove and parked the P-Wagon where she'd requested. I could already see her shadow moving about through her open blinds. I did a quick booger check in my rearview mirror before getting out of my car.

"What are you doing? Being chivalrous? I got this. Get back in there. It's only the one. Let's go. Pop the trunk." Nikki rolled a gigantic, overstuffed suitcase behind her.

"Getting it popping," I sang, pushing the open trunk button on my keys. I helped Nikki wrestle her suitcase into my car. "What's in here? A dead body?"

"Not yet." She wiped her hands together and shut the trunk. "Ready?"

"Yep."

She slid into the seat next to me, buckling up. "What is that smell? Something smells delicious! Is that bacon?"

"And eggs and bagels and muffins and also maybe a cake pop or five. And I hope you like tea, coffee, or hot chocolate." I nodded toward the backseat where the bags of food sat.

"Damn, Weston! How do you think I will eat all of that? Besides, that is spiked cholesterol in a bag!"

"Don't you know the best part about a road trip is the crap food? I'm just starting us off on the right foot, is all."

"I'm down for it. Now, where is that cake pop and bacon?" She reached behind her, grabbing a bag and rummaging through it. "I'm surprised you let anyone eat in your pussy wagon. Looks like a golden throne in here."

"It's just a car. I can buy another. Oh, before I forget. Here's that ring." I handed her the jewelry box I had tucked away in the middle console.

She licked the grease off of her fingers and slid the ring on, sticking her hand out and admiring the way it caught the light.

"You'd never know this was a fake! It's gorgeous!" She brought it up to her eye and peered down into it.

"That's because it's not a fake."

"What? You told me it was!"

"The one at the club was. This one isn't. My ma would be able to spot a fake."

"So, you're telling me, I have a big-ass real rock wrapped around my finger right now?"

*After our first kiss, that's not all you have wrapped around your finger, honey. Me and Dan. Me and Dan.*

"Yep." I pressed my lips into a thin line, tugging at my collar, and cleared my throat. "Ready to go over the plans one more time?"

"Relax! I got this. I'm a chef. We met at the taco truck when you were in town on business. I want lots of kids, and I like to bake cookies and shit. It's not that hard. I just have to pretend to be the perfect fifties housewife." She made a gagging noise with her throat and reached back for the drink tray.

"I take it, you don't want to be a housewife?"

"Do you think someone like me would want to be a housewife?"

"No. But a trophy wife, I do. I can see you lounging by the pool in a sheer fur-trimmed robe, sipping a mimosa and watching our old, fat pool boy clean the pool."

"Hate to break it to ya, Weston, but you don't know me at all then. My pool boy wouldn't be old and fat. He would be a ripped-up piece of beefcake."

"I know. I had to sneak the other in there. I can't be having competition for my role as a husband."

"Who says you would? A little side piece might not hurt anyone." She winked, reaching over to pat my knee.

"Do you really feel that way?" I pouted, already upset over my fake wife fake cheating on me with our fake pool boy.

"Hell no. And if you—or my future husband—ever pulled some cheating shit on me, I'd take a Louisville Slugger to your P-wagon. You can count on that." She sipped her coffee and leaned back in her seat, looking out of the passenger window.

"Thought so. See? I do know you. I notice you didn't turn down the mimosas and robe."

She side-eyed me and laughed. "It's been a long, hard life. I reckon I could use a little pampering and pleasuring after all I've been through. I think it's in the cards. Actually, I know it is. They told me so earlier this week."

"What do you mean, cards told you so?"

"Page of Pentacles. My tarot reader pulled it. It means I'm expanding my knowledge and wealth. So, maybe I'll learn how to bake cookies and shit after all. But also get rich, doing that."

"Like a housewife."

"Mutter that term to me again, and you're going to be that dead body I planned on packing in my suitcase. I was thinking more along the lines of Martha Stewart or someone with a cooking show or something. Not someone cleaning up after a man," she groaned, rolling her eyes.

"No, you wouldn't have to clean up after a man. You'd have your hot, sexy pool boy cleaning up."

"See? Now, you are getting to know me." She turned on the radio and raised the volume before leaning her head back onto the headrest and smiling.

I stroked Dan and lost myself deep in thought as we cruised toward the farm. I wondered how many men Nikki was juggling. Surely, someone as beautiful as she was had men falling at her feet. Hell, I was falling at her feet, and I barely knew her.

I knew she believed in spiritual stuff, ate lobster, had had a bad string of luck with exes who had gotten her into debt, could work a pole, kissed like someone out of a porn movie, and could make tacos. She was perfect. But she didn't seem to need me or any man in her life. I glanced over at the ring on her finger and willed it to stay.

I veered off the interstate toward an exit in a sketchy little town.

"Gotta pee?" Nikki asked, lowering her sunglasses.

"Nope. There's a place you might like here—fortune teller. We hire her out for our Halloween events at Westy's. She has a shop down here. Interested?"

"Hell yes!" Nikki's eyes grew wide as she bounced in her seat.

My head nodded in rhythm with her jiggly boobs, making her laugh.

"Okay. Hope she's open."

I drove a few blocks past liquor stores with barred doors, a cash-advance place that had boarded-up windows, and a diner that had a parking lot full of trash. I weaved through a few neighborhoods, searching out Fortune Teller Frannie's shop, which was also her house.

"Here we go!" I said, pointing at the painted purple brick shack.

A neon light that read *Open* hung in the window, but the black curtains were drawn.

"This looks amazing!" Nikki gushed, hopping out of the car as soon as I parked.

I followed behind her, up the crumbling concrete stairs, and knocked. I stepped in closer to Nikki, turning around and watching our backs. This area was known for crime, and the last thing I wanted to do was bring Nikki here to get hurt. I could handle myself. I'd once even tucked a teeny-tiny mace spray can inside Dan.

"Weston Banks! What are you doing here, son?" Frannie said, opening the door. "Come in! Come in!"

I held the door open, letting Nikki bounce past me through the beaded curtain and into a cloud of patchouli incense.

"Frannie, this here is my friend Nikki. She and I are on our way to the farm. I thought I'd stop in and check on you and show Nikki some of your work. She loves this type of stuff." I motioned toward the lava lamps, the hanging crystals, and a black cat with one eyeball that sat on a window ledge.

"Do you now?" Frannie turned toward Nikki.

"Yes, ma'am. It is all fascinating to me," Nikki replied, her eyes darting around the shop, gleaming.

"Good. Let's see what I can do for you today." Frannie reached out, grasping Nikki's hands in hers and closing her eyes for a brief moment before shaking her head. "Yes, child, I know. Come on. Weston, you stay here. I'll come back for you."

Nikki followed Frannie through another beaded curtain, still holding her hand. I paced the room before plopping myself down on a sunken-in green velvet chair next to the cat.

"Pleased to meet you, oh spiritual one," I told him.

He reached out with his paw, swatted Dan, and jumped off the ledge, disappearing into the back of the shop.

I gasped, offended at the crazy cat that was probably from the underworld.

"Good riddance, devil cat!" I said, crossing my arms and leaning back into the dusty chair.

I waited and waited. And then I waited some more.

I didn't mind waiting for Nikki. I figured whatever it was that was taking so long needed to be done. Not that I believed in any of this stuff.

"It's all just a bunch of hocus-pocus," I muttered under my breath, talking to myself again.

I rubbed my face with my palms and closed my eyes for a brief second, deciding that I might as well nap. The wind picked up outside just as I nodded off, rattling the shutters and sending me flying out of my seat, looking every which way for whatever ghost was playing tricks on me.

"You okay?" Nikki asked from the doorway, smirking.

"Yes. Just nodded off, is all." I straightened myself up.

"Your turn in there," she said, throwing her thumb back in the direction behind her. "I'll be right out here, waiting. Good luck."

"Good luck? What happened?" My voice hit a high pitch. "She wants to see me? I didn't come here for me. I think I'm good."

"She specifically told me to send you back. The second door on the right. Go get 'em, tiger!" Nikki reached out, smacking my butt as I walked past her and into whatever my future held.

I parted the beaded curtains and made my way down a dimly lit hall. The scent of patchouli grew stronger as I neared the room.

"Come on in, Weston. My third eye can see you puttering about out there," Frannie called.

I stepped through yet another beaded curtain and sucked in my breath. Frannie sat at a round table with a gigantic crystal ball in the center.

"It's just like the movies in here," I whispered, dodging the eighty candles surrounding the walls.

"Sit," Frannie commanded.

I lowered myself into the chair across from her, wringing my hands.

"I don't need any readings today, just so you know. I am good. Life is good. I—"

"The black cat told me what you did to him. Swatting his whiskers like that!"

My jaw dropped.

"He lies! He swatted Dan!"

"Who?"

"Not doing this again. He swatted my beard!"

"He said you told him you didn't believe in this hocus-pocus and you swatted him."

My pulse thumped throughout my eardrums as I began to break a sweat.

"Well"—I rubbed my hands down my pants—"I didn't say that exactly. Not to him. That black cat is trouble." I made the sign of the cross.

"Seems like you let a lot of trouble come into your life."

"What do you mean?" I asked.

My mind immediately went to Nikki. I wondered if Frannie was trying to send me a warning.

"I mean, this whole charade you are putting on for your parents so you can get the goods."

"Do I get the goods?"

"Which goods are we talking about here?"

"Nik—Westy's! Westy's," I blurted, dragging the back of my hand against my forehead before beads of sweat began to form.

Her hands reached out, rubbing the crystal ball back and forth.

"Oooommm," she called, tilting her head back and closing her eyes.

When she finally stopped chanting, she squinted into the crystal ball and gasped loudly, standing up so fast that her chair fell backward. I did the same.

"What? Oh no! What is it? Did I die?" I clutched my chest with one hand and steadied myself against the table with the other.

"Huh?" She peered into the crystal ball. "Oh, wait. That's not you. You're good."

"Oh, thank heavens!" I moaned, fanning my face.

"No. Wait. Do you … do you drive a pussy wagon?" she asked, moving her face closer to the crystal ball.

"Hells bells!" I cried out. "Do I crash it? Am I dying? Is Nikki okay?"

"No, no. It just looks sweet as fuck." She shook her head, picked her chair back up, and situated herself.

"I have to go. I can't handle this anymore. My blood pressure is through the roof. I don't want to know how I go!" I threw my hands in the air and backed away from the table. "Sorry, Frannie!"

"Now, listen here! You wait just a minute! I have something important that you need to know! Sit back down!" She pointed at my chair that still laid on the floor.

I overturned it and did as she'd said, terrified she would curse me if I didn't. "Please. I can't know anything serious. I would rather stick my head in the sand and go through life, clueless."

"Oh, you're clueless, all right," she sighed. "Now, blow this out." She stuck a candle in my face, to which I promptly huffed out.

"Why did I do that? Did I break a spell?" I breathed a sigh of relief.

"No, I just wanted to see if you'd do it."

"What for?" I cried.

"To prove a point."

"To?" I asked.

She raised a bony finger and pointed it toward the corner of the room, where a tiny television was tucked away. Nikki sat in the green velvet chair, waving and laughing. I had been on camera the entire time I waited on their session.

"You knew that black cat swatted Dan!" I cringed, realizing they'd watched me talking to myself too.

"It's the year 2020. Everyone has cameras. Don't you know I had to install them when some asshat was stealing from me while his mama came in here, getting her cards read?"

"So, you both tricked me. To prove what? That I'm gullible?" My face reddened.

My brother had been telling me all my life that I was a big, gullible dummy.

"Nope. To prove that one in there that she is more than a fake fiancée to you, so she needs to tread lightly."

"Can she hear us then?"

"Yes, I had the audio turned on, but it's switched off now. So, listen to me quickly before she comes back to get you. She has to tread lightly with that big heart of yours, but you have to tread lightly with hers too. You aren't just some fake fiancé to her either. I think you got a chance."

"Really? What did she say?" I twirled Dan around my finger.

"No time. Off you go!" Frannie stood up and shooed me down the hallway and out the door.

Nikki followed behind me, waving good-bye to Frannie.

I buckled myself into the P-wagon and took a moment to gather my bearings. I let out a loud sigh and started the car.

"No worries, Weston. The cat is long gone. You're safe with me," Nikki said, buckling in beside me.

"I think I'm more worried about you and your shenanigans than that devil cat," I muttered.

"I had questions I needed answered." She shrugged.

"And? Did you get your answers?" I asked.

"Yes. Did you get any answers?"

"Yes."

"Good. Now, let's go do our business," she said quietly. "Take me to your home, so I can do what I'm here for. Getting paid for sex work."

"What?" My eyes bulged out of my head.

"It's what you're expecting, aren't you? Sex? I'm assuming since I strip—thus working in the sex industry— that you are paying me to have sex. Fulfill all the fiancée duties, bedroom included. At least, that is what you think. That I can be some type of whore for you for the weekend. Remember, I warned you about that back at Scarlett Herb."

"What in the world? Where is this coming from? No, no, no! Not at all. I don't expect anything like that. What exactly happened back there in Frannie's shop?"

"Nothing. Look, I'm sorry. Some things were brought up back there that triggered me. You did nothing wrong. I'm here to pretend I love you. That's it." Her eyes glazed over.

My breath caught in my throat. "That's it," I agreed.

# FIVE

Nikki

"Holy cow! Literally!" I said, pointing at the cow walking across the gravel drive.

The car slowed to a stop to let the animal cross.

"That's Bessie!" Weston said, rolling down his window and letting out a loud *mooooooooo.*

The cow stopped in its tracks, looked toward the pussy wagon, and mooed back.

"Ha-ha! How did you do that?" I stuck my head out of the car and tried to moo back at it, but I swore that heifer rolled her eyes before trudging along.

"Just call me the cow whisperer. She told me everything I need to know in that one moo." He continued up the driveway.

At the top of the hill stood a plantation home like I'd only seen in the *Southern Living* magazines my mom had swiped from the barbershop. The red brick popped against a bright white mortar. An expansive porch circled both the top and bottom levels amid massive gothic columns.

"What did Bessie say?" I asked politely, though my eyes and mind were both distracted by taking in the mansion in front of me.

"She said, good luck winning over my ma and that she is in a spitfire mood today."

"Who? Your ma or the cow?"

"Both." He pressed his lips together and parked the car in front of the massive brick steps.

"Hey. It's going to be okay. I got this." I reached over, squeezing his hand. I flipped the visor down, looking over myself in the mirror. "I can handle Bessie and your ma—"

"Ma! Hi!" Weston shouted, drowning me out.

He hopped out of the car and rushed up the porch, greeting a lady who looked as if she'd stepped out of a '50s-era sitcom. Her powdered sugar–stained apron clung tightly around her waist, and her gray hair was loosely sitting atop her head in a messy bun. I opened my door and slowly pulled myself up to my full height, towering over this woman who was all of five feet, if that.

"Ma! I want you to meet Nikki, the love of my life," Weston spit out, pushing me forward and into harm's way.

"My boy! Finally settling down. And look at your hips. Those are some baby-making hips! Oh my gosh! I can't wait! Come here, hon! Give mama a hug!" Weston's mom stepped toward me and pulled me into her, squishing herself against me like a melted marshmallow. "You can call me Ma, or you can call me Jean. Your choice," she added, stepping back to take me all in.

"Thank you, Ma. This is such a lovely place you have here! Weston has told me all about it and all about you. I can't wait for you to tell me about him when he was little. You know, so I can figure out what our kids will be like." I winked, smoothing out my modest dress. I had this shit in the bag.

Ma clasped her hands together and beamed at the word *kids*. I felt a bit sad, leading this lady on. So far, she seemed super friendly. I had no idea why Weston was so worried about her.

"Now, let's get you in here in the kitchen and see what ya got! I've got to make sure you're good enough for my Weston. No one has ever measured up. I think you might be in luck though. We'll see!" Her voice rose to a shrill.

*Ah. There it is. Perfect son syndrome.*

I glanced at Weston, who looked like he was about to faint.

He leaned down to whisper in my ear, "Go on, I'll get the bags."

"Like hell you will! You aren't leaving me alone with her! Not yet anyway! Help me out a little at least!" I whispered back.

"Chop, chop!" His mom clapped her hands from the doorway where she stood, waiting. "We only have three days to get to know each other. I need all of that time alone just to see if I like you!" She laughed.

*Fuck.*

My blood pressure began to rise with each shrill syllable she sputtered out. I nodded toward her, narrowed my eyes at Weston, who turned to unpack the trunk, and made my way up to the gates of hell—according to Weston at least. The comment about being good enough threw me off, but I knew my worth, and I knew that I was not only good enough but damn worth it.

"Let's go, Ma! Got any cocktails in there we can get to know each other over?" I said, carrying myself up the stairs.

"Oh! Heavens no! We don't drink in this house!" she said, taken aback as if I had just asked her to help me bury a body.

A weekend with the Banks, and I couldn't even get slightly buzzed on booze. *Crap.* This whole trip was quickly beginning to feel more like a job. *Which it is*, I had to remind myself.

"I meant, sweet tea! That's what my girlfriends and I call it. Cocktails of tea. With a little lemon, and sometimes, we even add mint!" I smiled sweetly at her, giving her my best innocent eyes.

"Sweet tea I have by the gallon. Come on, dear. Let me get you a glass."

She opened the massive wooden doors and led me inside their farmhouse mansion. It looked exactly how I'd expected it to look—like a barn had thrown up in here. Pictures of cows, tractors, and chickens littered the walls. A giant iron rooster sat in the corner of the entry, holding a sign that said, *Welcome friends*. I shuffled behind Ma, afraid to touch anything. Not because it was nice, but because I didn't want to catch whatever sickness this was.

*Country life.*

Ma led me into a kitchen that was bigger than my first apartment. Plaid napkins, placemats, and dish towels were placed in every corner. Another damn rooster sat on the counter, offering up a plate of cookies. I couldn't help myself; I grabbed one.

"Sweet tooth, do ya? That's my special recipe. I keep them on hand every week. I call 'em cow patties because of how they look. Course they ain't cow patties!" She laughed, pulling out a chair and motioning for me to sit.

I took a bite out of the cow pattie and instantly tasted regret—regret for my waistline after I inhaled ten more.

"This is delicious! There is something in there that's unique. It's different. What gives it that sweet taste but with a twang?" I asked between mouthfuls of cookie.

"Balsamic vinegar. You have a good palate to taste that in there. Weston told me you worked as a chef?"

I cleared my throat, choking for a quick second on the cow pattie.

"Oh my! I didn't even get the tea out. I'm sorry, doll. Coming right up. My mind's not been right lately!" Ma hurried over to her refrigerator and took out the tea, pouring us two glasses.

I took the glass from her and drank it like I was downing tequila. I wondered if I could convince Weston to sneak away and buy us a bottle.

"Yes, I am a chef," I said, not sure how much Weston had told her.

"You cook tacos or something, right? Weston went on and on about it! Maybe you can make some while you're here. You teach me your taco secrets, and I'll teach you how to make a cow pattie! Better yet, if I like you … you'll get the family recipe book as a wedding gift."

I sucked in my breath and clutched my chest. "Really? You think I could? Weston has told me how much he loves his mama's cooking and how much he misses it. He said mine comes close, but nothing will ever compare to his ma. If I knew how he liked his food, I think that would make him so happy. I'd love to surprise him by making him a homemade meal from his childhood sometime!" I gushed.

Ma's face beamed with pride.

*Nailed it.*

"Oh, yes, ma'am, we will get you that! But not before the wedding. I've got to make sure you and my Weston are matched up properly. You know his last few relationships didn't work out so well. He's a good boy with a huge heart. He needs someone who can handle that big heart with care." Ma shook her head and took a sip of her drink.

"I agree! Poor thing has been treated so terrible with these ladies who snuck into his life! Ugh! Varmints!" I wrinkled my nose.

"You said it, sister. My boy's better than a shithouse rat!"

I gasped, "Ma! You are absolutely right! Shithouse rat!"

We laughed.

"What's this carrying on in here?" a man called from the doorway.

"Westy! Come meet our future daughter-in-law. Look at her hips! Aren't they some childbearing hips? Weston already told me he wants twelve!" Ma clasped her hands together as her husband made his way toward me.

"He picked a mighty fine one this time! Come on over here, sugar. I can't see very well. I need to make sure you have a button nose and all ten toes. Otherwise, you might taint the Banks' line."

He gently grabbed the end of my chin between his thumb and index finger, turning my face side to side. It was all I had in me not to punch this man in his face, inspecting me like that.

"Hey! Hey! Hey! She's not a new snow cone machine! You don't have to look her over that closely. She's perfect! That's my soon-to-be wife! You're inspecting her like a cow at a blue ribbon contest! Hands off, Dad!" Weston cried. His arms circled me as he brought me snugly into his chest. Dan tickled my forehead.

"Sorry, son. I trust ya. She does look something special."

"She is. Don't you all worry. Now, I'm assuming I'm in my old room?" Weston asked.

"You're in your old room, and I set up the second-floor guest room for Miss Nikki here. Can't have y'all shacking up before the wedding! That's bad luck! Follow me. I'll show you the way, so you can freshen up," Ma said, pulling my hand toward the stairs.

I shot Weston a look of death. His jaw muscle twitched as he waved me good-bye.

The rest of the evening went as expected. Weston's parents grilled me on my past, and I quickly made up a fairy-tale life that even I believed for a moment.

The whole time I spoke, Weston watched me, nodding and agreeing. He chimed in with, "Isn't she great?" and, "I'm so lucky," after nearly everything I said.

I was exhausted. Ma had me doing mental gymnastics the entire night. I would be lucky in the morning to remember what horseshit I'd fed to her. The way her eyes sparkled as I talked about my future with her perfect son did have me feeling a little bit of guilt. But the cash in my pocket that would set me on the path to financial freedom brought me back down to reality. Weston squeezed my leg under the table each time his mom asked me a question. The main points to remember about his family, Weston had told me in our drive up, were to talk about babies and wife stuff—like crafts, cleaning, and caretaking.

*Barf.*

I talked about children mostly, even going so far as to tell them the truth about some of what I did. I told them about my work at the cottage and how I'd spent time helping the disadvantaged youth. The passion in my voice came out when I spoke about my volunteer work. I had the entire Banks family teary-eyed at the dinner table.

"Sorry! I get a little carried away when I talk about the children." I set my napkin on the table. "That's enough of that! I think I'm getting sleepy." I yawned.

"That's okay, dearie. You are going to be an amazing mama." Ma reached across the table and squeezed my hand.

I smiled genuinely. This traditional Banks family thing wasn't so bad.

We finished dinner, skipped a nightcap due to their no-alcohol rule, and headed to bed.

"Now, you two kiss good night and be on your merry, *separate* ways. I'll see you both in the morning with my famous cinnamon rolls. It's going to be a long day tomorrow with party prep, and your brother and guests are arriving! Go get some rest!" Ma said, pushing herself up on her tiptoes to kiss Weston's cheek. She embraced me into her soft, squishy hug and patted my butt up the stairs.

"Can I help with the dishes?" I turned to ask her.

"Pfft! Not a chance. I have someone coming to clean in the morning. It's bedtime for all of us." She nudged Westy on the back, who had already fallen asleep at the table.

"Okay. Good night, Ma. Thank you for the lovely dinner," I said, following behind Weston up the stairs.

"Meet me in the bathroom. I got your pajamas," Weston whispered to me.

"Ten-four," I confirmed, shuffling my feet forward across the creaky floorboards.

I ducked into my room at the top of the stairs and grabbed my toiletry bag. I was ready for a hot shower and cozy pajamas. I tiptoed around upstairs, opening three doors before I found a bathroom, flipped on a light, and waited for Weston to give me my nightshirt so that I could sleep.

I turned the shower knob and began to let the water heat up, quickly brushing my teeth and slapping my face a few times to wake myself up.

"Here! Take these!" Weston poked a hand through the door, offering me my pajamas.

"You can come in. I'm decent," I said, opening the door and prying my pajamas from his hands. I unfolded black lacy thongs and straps that I assumed would cover just across my nipples. "Are you fucking kidding me?" I threw them at his chest. The lacy thongs caught in Dan and hung there, swinging back and forth.

"Yes, I am. Here. They match! Will be perfect for us going down to breakfast in the morning. Check them out. The lingerie you can keep for dancing at least, I thought." Weston shrugged his giant shoulders and handed me a bag.

I pulled out an oversize flannel onesie and sighed. "Whatever," I said, beginning to undress.

"Oh! I'll get out." He stepped back toward the door.

"Don't be silly! It's not like you haven't seen me half-naked before."

"I haven't seen your beaver!"

"Call it that again, and I'll make sure it gnaws your wood in half. If you're comparing my vagina to an animal, you'd better say it's a tigress or a leopard or a magical unicorn, but don't call it a beaver, or we'll have problems."

"Got it." He nodded. "I'll just step out and get ready for bed in the other bathroom. Let me know if you need anything else. Knock on my door at the end of the hall or text me. Have a good night, Nikki. You killed it down there. Especially with that cottage stuff. How did you come up with that?"

"That's really me. That one at least wasn't a lie," I whispered as I shut the door.

"You're amazing," he whispered back loudly through the door.

I smiled as I took a hot shower, dried off, and wiggled into my cozy flannel pajamas. It was too hot outside for flannel, but true to what Weston had told me, his mom had the air conditioner cranked down to a level that turned my nipples into glass cutters. I shivered as I wrestled myself into my onesie before realizing it had a butt flap. I turned around in the mirror, looking over my shoulder and cringing at the two buttons that held the flap shut.

I unfastened the buttons, laughed at my bare ass in the mirror, and left the flap hanging. When I opened the door to go back to my bedroom, Ma stood there, waiting with a fresh towel in her hand.

"Ahh!" I screamed, jumping nearly out of my skin.

"I thought you might like a fresh towel, dear. I couldn't remember if I had put any out or not," Ma said, handing me a fluffy towel with a horse sewn on it.

*Yeah, right. She wanted to see if I was shacking up with her innocent little boy.*

"Thanks. I found one in there. I appreciate it though. I'll just put this one right back where I found the other." I turned to shove the towel in the cabinet, not remembering my bare, panty-less ass hanging out the back of my pajamas. I froze as soon as I felt the draft from turning around quickly.

"Oh my! Dear! I think you forgot to adjust yourself after potty time." Ma covered her eyes.

"Sorry! I can't get used to these darn things. It's tough to button them up. I thought I'd just hold the flap up while I hightailed it to bed." I laughed, holding my pajamas together so I didn't expose any more of myself.

"I'll cover you." Ma looked both ways down the hall. "You got it! Run, run, run!" she whispered.

I yelped, holding my ass flap together against my cold buns, and skipped back to my room. I peeked out from behind the door and waved. "Night, Ma!"

But she was already walking down the stairs, shaking her head.

I snapped a selfie in the dresser mirror of my ass-less pajamas and sent it to DTF before turning off the light and tucking myself into my feathered bed. I pulled the covers over my shoulders and sighed happily. I was halfway to dreamland when I heard a quiet knock on my door.

*Damn it, Ma.*

I shuffled across the floor and unlocked the door.

"Did you forget something again?" I asked, opening the door to see that it was only Weston.

"No. I just wanted to see you in the pajamas I picked out. Check it out!" He turned around, showing me his buttoned-up flap covering his butt.

"Yeah, yeah. I noticed. I gave your mom a show too. Thanks. For the pajamas." I narrowed my eyes and made my way to shut the door, but he put his hand against the doorframe, stopping me.

"I came over because I wanted to thank you for being so wonderful down there. And I was wondering if maybe you were up for some talking. I could use some help with getting my mind off of tomorrow's big day. No telling what kind of stunt my brother will pull to get his name on everything!"

I rubbed my eyes and yawned. "Sure. Come on in. No promises I won't fall asleep though. I'm exhausted."

I opened the door. Weston ran inside and dived into the bed, bouncing on his knees.

"Slumber party!" he announced.

"No. This is me being nice and letting you tell me your feelings, so we can both get some sleep."

He sighed, lay down on the bed, and crossed his arms across his chest. "Oh, where do I begin? I think my troubles all started when I was four."

I crawled in bed next to him, propped myself up on my elbow, and prepared for a long night. "Mine started when I was four too. Go on."

"I was just kidding. I don't know when mine started. Probably the teenage years when my brother and I became competitive. He's not a total asshole or anything. I just want what I want, and that's not for him to run the family business. Only me. But now that you started on feelings, I want to know what started at four with you." He turned his body toward me and sat up on his elbow too. Dan was only inches from my face.

"I thought this was a conversation about you?"

"Not anymore. I don't want to relive it all. You tell me about you."

"Okay. I don't particularly like reliving mine either, but here goes. My dad left when I was young. My mom was never around. She worked odd jobs to make ends meet, and her free time was left with deadbeat boyfriends who didn't have jobs. They used her for her money, never paid any attention to me. Stole shit. Talked down to my mom and me. Did drugs. I had a lot of men coming in and out of my life. Now, I know my mom was only looking for love, but she forgot that she had it all along with me. I loved her, and I needed that love back. But she was gone, finding love from men. And I get that people don't want to be alone. But we don't need partners in life to make us happy. Hell, I'm happy with just having friends with benefits for now. Works for me," I rambled, feeling my blood pressure rise.

"I'm so sorry, Nikki. I can't imagine growing up, not having anyone to guide me really or not having a support system. You've done amazing for yourself. She missed out on you. Where is she now? Do you talk to her still?"

"It's not her fault. She grew up in a vicious cycle. Chaos was her normal. I get it now. But, no, she's not here anymore. She died six years ago. Breast cancer. That's why I cut mine off and filled my chest with fake ones. She had the gene, and so do I. We learned some tough lessons that last year, but it was too late. She was gone before we got to mend much. I don't fault her. She will always be my mama. I just wish she could have given me the family life I needed and wanted. Probably would have saved me some hard life lessons."

I rubbed my eyes, surprised at myself for getting so damn deep with Weston.

"And you don't want the family life anymore? You're happy being single and getting your needs met with *friends with benefits*, you said?" His brows pulled together.

"I don't know," I sighed. "It's not that I don't want all of that anymore. I've never had it. I guess I gave up on it because it's just … too late for me."

"Fiddlesticks! How old are you?"

"Twenty-eight."

"I'm thirty-four, and I'm not giving up on family life."

"But you have a family life."

"I know. But I want more. I want my own one day. Ten acres of land just like this here. I want to tell my grandkids to pull my finger while we ride on tractors and laugh at our five dumb dogs."

"You have this all planned out, don't you?"

"Yep."

"I hope you get what you want," I whispered, gently reaching out to stroke Dan before I knew what I was doing.

"I hope you find what you want." He smiled back at me, taking my hand and kissing my fingertips before sliding out of bed and disappearing into the night.

I stared at the ceiling and turned the celestite ring I wore on my index finger back and forth. My mom had given it to me right before she passed. She had told me it was known as the cosmic lullaby crystal. She had asked that when I wear it, I should think of how she would forever sing me lullabies to make up for all those nights she'd missed singing them while here on Earth. Despite our rocky relationship, I never took off my celestite ring.

# SIX

Weston

"Rise and shine, dear!" my ma called, tapping on my door. "Breakfast is gettin' cold! Hurry down!"

I rubbed my eyes and let them adjust to the sunlight streaming through my window. I had woken up in the middle of the night, nervous over the big day. I knew my parents would keep me busy enough to keep my mind off of it, but I didn't want to leave Nikki alone with my family—especially Wes.

I groaned like an old man as I pushed the blankets off of me and rolled out of bed. Today was the day that my entire family would meet my fake fiancée, and I needed to prepare myself. I jogged in place for fifteen seconds and did half a push-up and two jumping jacks to get my blood flowing. When I bounced in place, my flannel pajamas rubbed scratchily against my stubbled manscaping, reminding me that I had gotten too carried away with that damn razor. I tugged the elastic waistband and peered down between my legs. Razor burn dotted my entire nether regions.

*Ouch!*

I stuck my hand down my pants and itched around my balls. When I had shaved myself smooth yesterday, I never thought about the aftermath of growing sandpaper back. I opened my bedroom door and hobbled to the bathroom in hopes of finding something, anything, I could use to give me some relief. I itched, I burned, and I cursed my dick.

"What are you doing?" Nikki laughed, stopping me in the hall and catching me with my hand still down my pants.

"Nikki!" I yelped. "Good morning." I reached my hands up above my head as if I were being held up.

"You can put your hands down, silly. I'm not arresting you for scratching your johnson."

I winced, nodding and shuffling my feet inside the bathroom.

"Be right back," I croaked.

"Are you okay? You don't look so good. Did you … sleep on your penis wrong or something? Is that a thing?"

"No, no. I … had a mishap. With a razor." I cupped my dick, whimpering.

"You cut your dick?" she gasped.

"Shh! No! Golly, if Ma heard you say that, we would be in a pickle! No, I didn't cut my dick! I got carried away in the shower when I was doing my manscaping yesterday, and I shaved everything clear off! Now, I'm paying for it."

"Why would you shave it all off?"

"Because I have sascrotch! That's why! I'm a woolly mammoth! Think Dan is just confined to my chin? Think again," I blurted, putting my burly shame out there for her to take or leave.

Her eyes crinkled. "Sascrotch? So, you're trying to tell me you're a manly man then. Not some smooth-shaved city boy." She stepped closer to me.

"I guess you can look at it that way. Except now, I'm a stubbly porcupine who needs to change out of this flannel and into nothing because my balls are rubbed raw, and I itch like the dickens." I stuck both hands down my pants and went to town, scratching, groaning in relief.

"The dickens?" She laughed. "Calm down there. Let me grab some coochie cream, and you'll be good to go. You might need to slather yourself up a few times today though. Also, your cock is going to smell like cotton candy."

Nikki ran into her room and came back out with a small bottle of lotion, dangling it in my face. "Take it. It helps. I learned the hard way, being a stripper. You have to be pretty much hairless. I should buy stock in this stuff. Anyway, see you at breakfast!" She turned around and left for downstairs.

"Thanks, wifey," I croaked, shutting the bathroom door and lubing up every inch of my botched manscape. Butterflies fluttered around in my stomach as I wondered why she had brought coochie cream to my parents' house.

By the time I made it to breakfast, my balls had quit burning, and I could walk straight. The smell of bacon, my ma's special cinnamon rolls, and coffee had been enough motivation for me to fly down those stairs and join my family circus.

"Good mornin'!" I said, bending down to kiss my ma, who was pouring Nikki a cup of coffee. "And good mornin' to my beautiful wife-to-be too!" I kissed Nikki's forehead.

"I trust ya slept okay?" Ma said, grabbing another mug.

"I did. Here, sit down. I got it. Let me serve you!" I insisted, pulling out a chair for my overworked mother.

Nikki smiled. Her eyes followed me as I fixed my ma a plate before going back to make my own and settling down.

"He is just perfect, isn't he? You know, you can judge a man by the way he treats his mother," Nikki said, taking a bite out of her cinnamon roll.

The sticky icing rolled down her bottom lip before she wiped it away and licked her finger … slowly. I couldn't tear my gaze away from her.

"He has always been the sweeter one. Not to say Wes isn't sweet. He is too. But he is more push and shove, and my Weston here is more of a step aside," Ma said, patting my back.

Nikki caught me watching her and winked, sucking on her finger again.

*What in the world? Does she want my body? Does she think I'm sexy?*

The song popped into my head as her little cocktease gave me newfound motivation.

"Well, it's easy to step aside and be a gentleman when you are surrounded by lovely women," I said.

"Yeah, not like that lizard lady you dated!" Dad said, grabbing a plate and sitting down beside me.

Nikki's eyebrows shot up into her hairline. I never told her about the lizard lady for apparent reasons.

"Yep, yep." I cleared my throat. "So, what time is everyone supposed to be here?" I pushed the food around on my plate.

"Your brother's supposed to be here just after lunch," Ma said. "But everyone else should be arriving around six. Caterers should be set up by then. The band starts at seven and the fireworks at nine. Lord willing, everyone should be out by midnight!"

"Sounds like a fun party!" Nikki said, smiling over at me.

"It's the best! We do it every year. You'll see. Maybe by this time next year, you'll have a baby in your belly, and I'll be a grandma!" Ma clapped.

"Lord willing," Nikki replied, not missing a beat.

"Can I help you clean up, Ma?" I asked, finishing my plate and taking it to the sink. I grabbed Nikki's and took it to the sink too.

"No, sweetie, you may not! The cleaning crew helped a bit this morning. They're cleaning our room right now but will be back to help me shortly. You just show that pretty bride of yours around. Take her out on the tractor and show her the farm." Ma reached across the table to pat my hand.

"Tractor shmactor. Take her on the four-wheeler to the mud pit," Dad said.

"Mud pit?" Nikki squealed. "Can we, Weston? Please, please, please!"

"Well, if you insist. I hope you've got some clothes with you that you don't mind getting dirty," I replied. I hadn't been mudding since that one night in college when I drank too much Jack Daniel's and danced naked as a jaybird in a puddle. That was the latest mudding experience I'd had, which had sworn me off of mud—and Jack—ever since.

"Let's go! I've got something I can wear," she said, hopping up out of her seat, thanking Ma for breakfast and kissing her cheek before taking off upstairs.

"I reckon that bride of yours has a wild streak in her." Dad grinned. "Reminds me of your mama."

"Oh, you! Hush!" Ma cast her eyes away and blushed.

This was beginning to be awkward territory.

"All right. I'll just step out and be back around lunchtime. See ya! Thanks for breakfast!" I backed away from the kitchen and ran upstairs.

Nikki was already in her room with the door shut. The thought of her back at the table, licking those lips, sent my willy jumping in my pants. Just knowing that she was on the other side of that door, naked, had me all riled up. I stopped right outside of her door, hesitating on if I should knock or not.

"What are you doing?" she blurted, opening the door so fast that a mad rush of wind slapped me in the face.

"How did you know I was out here?" I asked.

"Because you sound like a Clydesdale walking up the steps. Now, where is this mud wrestling going to happen?" She stepped out of her room in only a tightly fitted white tank and a pair of jean shorts.

"I, uh … I—what—shorts."

She cringed. "Yes. I am in shorts. You should be too. It's not like you haven't ever seen these before!" She pulled the neckline of her tank down, letting her boobs pop right out in the open.

"Bra!"

"No … no bra. Do I need to speak in caveman terms too? You, Weston. Take me, Nikki. Mud. Now," she said.

I nodded, unable to speak.

She stuck her foot out to the side, crossed her arms, and sighed, "Do I need to dress you too?"

I kept nodding.

"Fat chance at that. Get you and Dan in your room and get dressed. I'll meet ya downstairs."

I shuffled my feet down the hall toward my bedroom and slipped into a pair of shorts. I rubbed my palms together, realizing that Nikki would be sitting with her legs spread behind me, hanging on to me. She would have to put her arms around me to not fall off the four-wheeler. It was required.

I hopped down the stairs two at a time, throwing my arms out in a perfect landing, right at the feet of my ma and Nikki. I walked right over to Nikki, put my arms around her, and dipped her, kissing her right on the mouth.

Her eyes flew open, but she didn't stop me.

"Weston!" Ma shook her head. "Here. I packed you up a picnic." She handed me a basket.

"Your mom is the best, Weston! Thank you, Ma." Nikki hugged her before turning toward the door.

"Be back soon!" I called, grabbing Nikki's hand.

We made it across the front yard and into the big barn before she said anything.

"You kissed me!"

"Well, you're my bride. Of course I did!" I shrugged, stifling a laugh.

"Weston Banks! You know I'm your fake bride! You can't go kissing a fake bride!"

"I'm sorry. I know. I was just trying to make it real. And honestly, I watched you eat breakfast, and the way you licked that frosting off your lips earlier … wowie! I can't shake that look you gave me. Hop on." I slapped the seat of the four-wheeler.

"It's fine. It felt pretty good actually. It's been a while since I've been touched like that. No passion or dipping my back and kissing me as you did. Most of my fun is a one and done and then get the hell out."

"They tell you to get the hell out? That is terrible!" I said, wrestling to secure the picnic basket on the back of our ride.

"No. I tell them to get the hell out."

I swung my leg over the four-wheeler. "So, how many of these *friends* do you have?"

"Enough to keep me satisfied when that craving hits but not too many that I have to deal with all their shit constantly," she answered, straddling in behind me. The heat from between her legs rubbed up against the tip of my butt, instantly thickening my dick.

"Is that a lot?"

"Are you slut-shaming me or just curious?"

"Wondering how much competition I have, is all."

"Oh, husband," she sighed, putting her arms around me and laughing.

I revved the engine on the four-wheeler and took off around the property. With every bump in the yard, I felt her rub up against me. I had gotten as hard as a rock before we even made it out of the barn. She held on tight as I veered away from the chickens and toward Bessie, so I could stop and let her pet Ma's moody cow.

"Have you ever tipped her?" Nikki narrowed her eyes down at me as she gently stroked Bessie's back.

"Of course not! I would never do such a thing!" I gasped, patting the heifer on the rump.

I averted my eyes. I had totally tried to tip Bessie over when I was younger. I wanted to impress my friends, but cow tipping was a whole lot harder than I had thought. Somehow, I ended up on top of Bessie, racing full speed down the driveway. Riding a cow was not like riding a horse. I'd left Bessie alone after that.

"Mmhmm," she hummed, still staring me down.

I motioned for her to hop back on our ride, quickly changing the subject. "Come on. Let's get to the lake, creek, and mud pit. There's a lot to see if we want to be back around lunch!"

We started back up toward the lake as I pointed out the spot for the fireworks and the field where everyone would park their cars. Already, tents were being erected and tables set up. My family didn't know the meaning of a small gathering. Every Banks party was over the top. One time, we had even hired Santa and his reindeer for Christmas. Unfortunately, Santa had been a mean drunk, and his reindeer had had the shits, but it was memorable at least.

I circled the lake before heading toward the meadow that led to the mud pit. The tall grasses brushed past us as we bounced our way to the creek. Nikki's boobs jostled against my back. She couldn't see the wide, goofy grin that played across my face each time I felt a nipple bounce.

"Faster! *Ándale!*" she shouted behind me, cracking a fake whip.

"Think you can handle it?" I shouted back.

"Ha! Do you even know me?"

I pushed the pedal down even further and took us flying across the fields. Nikki's arms tightly death-gripped around me, causing me to have trouble breathing. She could probably outmuscle me.

"Is this fast enough?" I croaked.

"That's more like it! Woohoo!" she screamed.

I threw in a few wild turns, made some doughnuts with my tires, and tried my best to drift into a shaded parking spot but failed miserably. My attempt at showing off only crashed us into a tree.

"Are you okay?" I panicked, turning around and patting her all over, making sure she was still in one piece.

"What the hell are you doing? Yes! I'm fine. Don't quit your day job to become a race car driver though." Nikki brushed off her shoulders and reached for the basket.

"Here, I got a blanket." I opened the back compartment and pulled out an old quilt.

"Do you do this often? Picnic and blanket?"

"My parents do. Why do you think my dad suggested the four-wheeler? My parents are freaks!"

"No way! Your mom seems like the sweetest, most innocent woman ever. I don't even know what you were worried about, bringing me here."

I fluffed out the quilt, laying it down under the shade tree I'd crashed into.

"They're ridiculously kinky. I once found a box in their closet when I went snooping for my Christmas presents. Let's just say, I never snooped again." I shuddered.

"What did you find?" Nikki sat down on the blanket and began unpacking the basket.

My mom had loaded it with sweets, fruits, olives, cheeses, and sparkling cider.

"Some kind of dinosaur dildo. Or wait, it was a dragon one, I think! Yeah! It was like a huge dragon claw that vibrated. There were three of them! And all sorts of porn stuff. Nipple clamps too! And lots of stripper-type lingerie and heels!"

"Wow! You really went through all of that stuff?"

"I was a kid. Of course! It was burned into my brain forever! It makes me ill to think about it." I grabbed a plate and loaded it with food. I still felt full from breakfast, but I wasn't about to pass up a picnic with one of the most beautiful women I'd ever laid eyes on.

"That sounds horrifying. But moms need love too. Speaking of love, I think I'm in love—"

My heart skipped a beat as I started to cough, choking on an olive.

"With your mom," Nikki finished, curiously eyeing me.

"Really? But she makes us sleep in separate bedrooms and doesn't pack us wine! Look!" I held the sparkling cider up and poured it into plastic cups.

"And?"

"She is overbearing as fuck! You've met her! She wants me to do this and that and have babies and be a good boy and blah. It's overwhelming!"

"I see a mom who bakes cookies for her favorite son. I mean, she basically said you were her favorite earlier. And she does all the fun mom stuff. She takes care of you. She loves you. She's there for you. She's pushing you to have grandbabies because she will be an amazing grandma. Just think, yes, it's stressful, but she won't be here forever. Might as well soak up all the love and family life you can now. People can disappear out of your life without a moment's notice."

"I'm sorry, Nikki. You're right. I don't know what it's like to not have a family. I shouldn't complain." I shrank into the blanket, realizing that maybe I was coming off as a douche bag.

"Not everyone gets to have a caring family. I sure didn't, and the kids I work with at the cottage rarely even see their parents. Sometimes, they don't even come home. And these are children! Most of them are teens, but some of the kids are as little as six years old and foraging their bare pantries for days before their mamas show up. Dads? Forget it. It's very rare for a dad to be in the picture at all."

"Jeez. Fuck. Six years old?" My brows pulled together, and shame bubbled up in my chest.

"Hey. It's okay. You haven't had experience with that side of life. Good for you. Really, I'm not trying to be snarky. That's great. You're privileged, is all. I'll bring you to the cottage sometime, so maybe you can understand my perspective on your 'overbearing family,'" she said, making air quotes.

*Privileged. I'm privileged. Fuck!*

"I would love to meet your children and learn some more about what you do. I can tell you're passionate about it." I tried to smile at her, but all I could find in myself was a shaky pout.

I never had anyone put my life into perspective before. My life had been surrounded by mostly good things. I never lacked for much of anything, except a love life. I had more money than I needed, but I never acted like a snob about it. At least, I hadn't thought I did until I began to think about my supportive family life versus the way Nikki had told me she had grown up. I cringed.

"It's okay. I can see I ruined our fun mood. Cheer up. I can't relate to you, and you can't relate to me. But your parents are golden. Just remember that," she said, patting my hand and popping an olive into her mouth.

She lay back onto the blanket and looked up at the sky.

"That one's totally a penis." She pointed to a cloud floating by.

I turned my face to the sky. "What? That is not a penis!" I laughed, lying down beside her, pushing her deep thoughts into the back of my mind. "Now, that one over there, that might be a penis." I pointed to a sad little cloud hanging out in the distance.

Nikki laughed, forcing herself up on one elbow and looking at me. She tugged at Dan and smiled. "You're fun, Weston. And you're a really good man."

"So are you, Nikki. Uh, fun, I mean. Not a man. Anyway, I'm sorry for not realizing what an ass I must sound like, complaining about an overbearing family when I have all of this." I put my hands in the air, motioning around the property.

"Like I said, it's okay! Forget about it. Don't beat yourself up. We are all constantly growing and learning. You've just never had a trailer-trash bride to get shit real for you!" Nikki laughed, tugging at my arm. "Now, show me this creek and mud pit! Let's wrestle this white male privilege out of you."

"Fuck, I'm so, so sorry." I mentally smacked my head against a wall.

"Ha-ha! I'm just fucking with you. Sort of." We pulled each other off the blanket and walked toward the creek.

Nikki stopped at the edge, closed her eyes, and took a deep breath.

"Serenity," she whispered over the bubbling of the water. Her hand reached out to touch a stone, disrupting the current. "If I were you, this is what I would want my parents to sign. The deed to this place. Fuck Westy's, the hotel, the diner. I would want this."

I nodded my head, stopping long enough for once in my life to listen to the water, the birds, the wind. I never paid much attention to that sort of stuff.

"You're about to get your feet wet. Come on, darlin'." I held her hand as we skipped over rocks to the other side of the creek and to the top of a hill. Down below was the mud pit, as sloppy and muddy as I'd ever seen it.

"Oh my gosh!" she squealed, taking off her shoes and running toward the mud.

"Wait! Are you sure? It's about a foot, maybe two feet deep!" I called after her, hesitating.

"It's Mother Earth! Of course I'm sure! It's not like you're jumping into a frying pan! It's mud!" She laughed, scooping up a glob of it in her hands and flinging it at me.

A fat clump of mud hit Dan before slowly dribbling off. Nikki clutched her sides, laughing and falling back on her ass, straight into the mud. She tossed her head back, gasping for breaths between laughter.

"You know you're going to pay for that one!" I shook my head, brushing the mud out of Dan. I took off my shoes and scuffed my foot across the dirt like a bull, revving myself up. "Bombs away!" I yelled, running toward Nikki at full speed and jumping into the mud.

I pounded my feet into the cold goo, sending it flying everywhere. There was mud in her hair, her mouth, and on poor Dan.

"You little shit!" She laughed, pulling me down to her and wrestling me to the ground.

She climbed on top of my lap, facing me with wild eyes and a wicked grin. My heart raced as I contemplated her next move. She was either about to drown me or bite my head off. I winced. She took the back of my head in her hand, steadied herself with the other, and pulled me in for the dirtiest kiss I'd ever had. Mud smeared across our lips, chin, cheeks as we made out like teenagers in the middle of filth.

"How do you like that?" she panted before putting her lips back on mine.

"I love Mother Earth," I whispered into her mouth, dazed.

My head swam with the possibility that some animal might have pooped in here, and I could have a smeared turd or slimy bug or something on my lip, but the way Nikki had kissed me had me out of fucks.

"Good. I do too. Chase me, and I might let you catch me. But if you do, I want to be dipped and kissed again as you did in front of your mama. Except, this time, no one is watching."

Nikki rose to her full height and took off running toward the creek.

"I think she is flirting with us, Dan," I whispered, watching her ass bounce as she left.

I hurled myself to my feet, slipping once, twice in the mud before catching my footing, my bearings, and my emotions. Just kidding, my feelings were all over the place. I had already started falling for Nikki the second I watched her cream-pie the stage. And with every kiss we'd had since, I kept falling harder and harder.

I ran down the hill and into the creek, splashing toward her as she dashed away again, farther down to where the stream deepened. I trudged through the water, like a hunter tracking its prey. She turned to check how far behind I was and gasped as I launched myself at her.

"Wow! You're like the big, bad wolf—"

I came up behind her, scooping her into my arms and kissing her like I'd seen those passionate men do it on all those Hallmark movies my ma had me watch at Christmastime.

Nikki's body relaxed into my arms as she pulled her head away and whispered, "I didn't think I could top that serenity and peace I'd felt earlier, but you might have just given it some competition. Because now, I'm peaceful—and horny."

My mouth dropped open. "Oh? Oh! Well, I, um … I …" I looked around for a place to set her and give it to her good. We were both caked up to our ears in mud. "I'd say, let's rinse you off in this creek, but then the pee fish will get to you. Can't have that!"

"Excuse me?"

"The pee fish. If you're naked in the water, a fish swims up your pee hole and lives in there."

"Are you fucking kidding me?"

"I swear, I saw that on TV one time, and I've never been naked in a creek since! Come on. Let's get you home and cleaned up." I wiggled my brows.

"Weston, I don't think there's pee fish in here." She laughed. "But I'll not take the chance. Maybe we can come back another time. I'll just go take a cold shower and get all of this mud off of me anyway." She wiggled down from my arms.

"Okay," I said in a low voice.

I'd once again put my foot in my mouth and ruined another moment that could have gotten me laid by my fake fiancée, who I was falling in love with. She would have been worth all the pee fish in the world.

I sighed, "Let's go back home. This mud is starting to dry and feel tight anyway." I cringed, pulling at my shorts and solemnly heading back to the house, sans nooky.

# SEVEN

*Nikki*

When we arrived back at Weston's parents' house, an old neon-green hippie van with flower decals painted on the sides sat parked at the front entrance.

"That's not something I see every day," I said, squinting my eyes to make sure I wasn't hallucinating.

"Doesn't have shit on the P-wagon," Weston said, revving up the four-wheeler and pulling it around to the barn.

"Whose is it?" I asked.

"My brother's." Weston grew silent as he parked our ride and hopped off.

"You don't speak of him much, but I get the feeling that you two aren't close. Which, by your eclectic taste in vehicles, I find pretty weird. Seems like y'all would be best buds."

"We are friendly. But a little competitive, and I think our relationship has suffered from this whole passing-on-the-business stuff." Weston took my hand in his. "Come on. I guess you'll have to meet him sometime."

The sadness in his voice ever since we'd left the creek was upsetting, even for me. I wasn't the type to get dragged down into other people's abysses. But the way he slumped his giant shoulders and stuck his pouty bottom lip out broke my heart.

I checked in with myself and let those thoughts roll around in my head as we silently walked back toward the farmhouse.

*I'm feeling for Weston. I feel for Weston. I have the feels for Weston?*

My lips curled under my nose as I realized my flirtatious behavior at the mud pit wasn't only because I'd felt like getting sexy, but also because I actually liked Weston Banks, the biggest goofus I'd ever met.

Weston stopped and lowered his voice. "Hey! Are you okay?"

"Yeah, yeah. Sure. Better than okay. We're going to rock this. I got you." I smiled.

*Get it together, bitch. Get it together.*

His hand fell on my lower back, gently nudging me up the porch and back inside. The heat from his touch seared up my spine, causing the hairs on the back of my neck to stand on end.

*Weston Banks*, I thought while rubbing my palms on my temples.

We slipped off our muddy shoes at the door and tiptoed our way inside.

"Mercy me!" Ma called from the bottom of the stairs. "You two did get in that mud! Goodness gracious!" She shook her head.

Beside her stood a short man with a beard just as long as Weston's. I wondered if he'd named his beard too.

"Well, go get cleaned up, you two, but first, let me introduce you. Say hi to Wes and his fiancée, Kristy," Ma said, motioning toward a mousy-looking woman who'd just stepped out of the kitchen. Her mouth was full of Ma's cow pattie. "Kristy and Wes, this is Weston and

Nikki. There, y'all can catch up later before you get mud all over the floors!" Ma continued.

"Nice to meet you!" I smiled at the couple.

The woman stuck her nose in the air and sighed.

"We'll catch up, brother. I would love to get to know how you and your *fiancée* met," Wes said before turning and disappearing into the kitchen with Kristy.

Weston's nostrils flared. I reached for his hand and pulled him into the bathroom, turning on the shower to drown out my whispers.

"You didn't tell me I had competition!" I huffed.

"I didn't know! That little weasel!" Weston curled his hand into a fist and shook it in the air.

"It's all right. We've just got to up our game. We have to convince your parents that we're in love and going to carry on the family name."

"I've been trying! What more can I do?"

"Shower with me."

"What in the world? I mean, yes, of course, that is the answer!" Weston stripped his shirt off, tugged his shorts down halfway, and paused.

"That was easy. But I'm asking you to shower with me, so we can get intimate. Not intimate sexy time, but know each other. Get closer. If we are going to pull this off, we need to know each other inside out. Plus, you've seen me half-naked already. It shouldn't be a big deal. For you." I grinned.

I was horny as fuck, and this was my only move. Luckily, Weston was gullible enough—or horny enough— to fall for it.

"It's a big deal for me. I have to tell you something." Weston pulled his shorts back up to his hips and chewed his bottom lip.

"I knew it! You have a vagina! You were way too nice to have a cock and balls." I leaned against the sink and crossed my arms.

"No. No vagina here. But … I'm different."

"You … what does that mean?" The alarms going off in my head drowned out the pulsing that had been going on between my legs.

"I'm uncut," he sighed, putting his head in his hands.

"Oh. Well, that's okay." I took his hand and pried it off his face so that he could look at me. "You know that is what they are originally supposed to look like anyway, right?"

"I know. But it's not common, and I didn't want to just spring it on you when it … sprang at you."

"You have nothing to worry about. I'm judgment-free, and I prefer things as natural as Mother Earth made them. That includes you. Now, strip down and let me get the mud off of you." I snapped my fingers and pointed at his shorts.

*Knock, knock, knock.*

"Yoo-hoo! I hope you're just washing your hands in there! No funny business before the wedding! That's bad luck. You can't buy the cow if the milk is free!" Ma called from the other side of the door.

*What the fuck?*

I winked at Weston, whispering, "Another time. Go get clean. I got this."

I opened the door and slid out, leaving Weston half-dressed and pouty yet again.

"I was helping warm up the shower for him like a good soon-to-be wife. He did sneak a kiss though! Such a charmer!" I giggled. "I've got to gather my things before showering anyway. I plan on being at my best for the party!"

Ma eyed me up and down. "You're a doll. I'm so happy Weston picked you. To be honest, that Kristy rubbed me the wrong way. Watch out with that one," she said, shaking her head and heading back downstairs.

I immediately rushed to my phone that I had left on the nightstand. I knew DTF would be together today. This evening was poetry night at The Lounge, and those days, we usually spent the afternoon together too. It had become a tradition lately. I swiped through my phone and pressed the number for Rox.

"It's the bride-to-be! How is life over there, Ms. Fancy Pants?" Rox answered on the second ring.

"Crazy. I guess that is what in-laws are known for though! I've got a problem. I need DTF to solve my … dilemma. I'm kind of in freak-out mode," I whispered into the phone.

"Why don't you consult your crystals?" Betty called.

"Okay, guess I'm on speakerphone. Glad I didn't have any secrets!" I huffed.

"We don't do secrets. You know that, silly. What is your dilemma? Can't decide if you love Weston or not?" Layla chirped.

*That's weird. How did she know I was catching feelings?*

"No. Gosh, it's a business arrangement. Which, saying that, I'm about to be a hypocrite. Fuck it. Here goes. He's not circumcised. What do I do with it?" I quietly panicked into the phone.

"I knew it!" Layla snorted.

"Knew what? That he isn't cut? How can you tell? Does it change the shape of their real head too? I've never been with an uncut man. Help! I'm clueless!" I pleaded.

"No, I meant, I knew you liked him!" Layla laughed.

"You don't know that. Nikki can screw a man she doesn't like. We all can. It's called getting our needs met," Betty groaned. "Now, look, what the hell do you mean, what do you do with it? You do what you always do with it. The only difference is, it looks different. Ever seen one?"

"Not up close and personal!" I paced the floor of my bedroom, tracking dried mud crumbs across the rug.

"Don't let it scare you. It's going to look like it's fat with a little head. But that is how it's supposed to look. They are usually thicker than a cut man, so you get that advantage. Also, they don't lose a lot of sensation like a cut man. So, that is his advantage. Also—" Betty continued.

"Fat with a little head. Got it! It did look thick in his pants!" I giggled.

"Just do what you normally do, and you'll be fine," Rox chimed in.

"So, I don't have to, like, pull anything back with my hand or my mouth or wiggle it a certain way or anything like that? How does a condom not slip off of that? If the skin is all wiggling?" I asked.

Layla laughed loud enough in the background that I had to hold the phone away from my ear.

"This is beyond my brain cells, so I know it's light-years beyond yours, Layla! I don't know what is so funny! I'm going into this blindly. I won't have my usual tricks if I don't know what the fuck I'm dealing with!"

"Crystal Cream Pie can handle it. Just put it in your mouth and do your thing! Don't go stretching skin out or poking at it!" Betty groaned.

"And you're sure? That's it? Treat it like a normal one?" I bit my lip, imagining just how that would work. I was still confused about the whole situation, but if I wanted to get laid, I didn't have a choice.

"Yes! It's the exact same." Rox laughed.

"It is. She's right. You know when you are putting on a turtleneck, and your head pops out the top and—" Layla started.

I hung up the phone and shot a quick text to Rox to tell them all thanks, but I had to run. I was not going to hear Layla's opinion. She was rooting for Weston and me, and all I wanted was to fill this empty ache between my legs—or so I told myself.

I busied myself upstairs for over an hour, washing and blowing out my hair, making my makeup flawless, squeezing into a sexy yet modest dress. Weston had gone downstairs to help with the party prep after his shower. Though I didn't know what he could help with, as by the time I got out of the shower, teams of people were running around everywhere, setting up for the big night.

I looked out of my bedroom window and marveled at the area around the lake. Big white tents were set up and filled with tables and decorations. A dance floor had been constructed in one of them along with lighting and deejay equipment. I had seen these types of things at weddings but never at a family party.

*Damn, they're loaded.*

I peeled myself away from the window, ready to face the competition downstairs. Weston had picked the right woman to stay by his side. I would give him that. I was competitive as fuck. And now, standing up against Kristy and Wes, my drive to win his parents over had increased tenfold. I slipped on my heels, tipped my chin up, and smirked. I was going to get my fake man his dream.

I tiptoed downstairs and made my entrance into the kitchen, all fresh-faced and smiles.

"Hello again!" I smiled at Kristy. "Where did the boys take off to?" I asked Ma, who was elbow deep in a ball of dough.

"Shenanigans. They're probably into shenanigans! Messing with them fireworks, I suppose," Ma huffed.

Kristy's laugh echoed off the walls, stopping me in my steps. She sounded like a choking sea lion.

"Ha! Shenanigans. That Wes! He is trouble!" She fanned herself as she sat at the table, watching Ma.

I walked to the sink, washing my hands and drying them before sidling up next to Ma. "Well, let's hope they don't get into too much trouble! Now that I won't get mud in your meals, what can I help with? Let me work too."

"Such a dear. Do you know how to roll out a pie crust?"

"Yes, ma'am, I do. I often make my own cream pies. Did Weston tell you about them? He loves my cream pies." I smiled sweetly.

Kristy guffawed again.

"Is something wrong, Kristy?" Ma asked.

Kristy looked at me to save her, but I played dumb.

"No. Sorry, I was laughing at something I remembered from earlier. Wes was making jokes in the van, and that man is just the most darling. I'd love to have ten of his babies." Kristy sighed into her sweet tea.

*Great. She is playing the game too.*

"How did y'all meet?" I narrowed my eyes.

"Oh! It's the sweetest story, y'all! I was outside, helping an elderly lady across the street, when I saw this old van pull up. Wes hopped out and helped the old lady across the street for me. He told me he thought I was so kind and thoughtful to stop and help someone in need and asked for my number right then and there. The rest is history!"

*Classic.*

"What about you? How did you and Weston—" Kristy started.

"Morning, ladies!" Weston shuffled through the doorway, interrupting her.

"There're my boys!" Ma beamed.

Wes sat next to Kristy, putting her face in his hands and kissing her. Her back became rigid, and her hand curled into a fist.

"I hope you two haven't been into any trouble," I said, working the pie dough between my hands.

"Not at all. Just tipping ol' Bessie out there since you gave me the idea earlier." Weston grinned.

"I did no such thing!" I laughed, rolling a tiny ball of dough and tossing it at him.

He caught it midair—in his mouth. I laughed again while he grinned at me like he had just accomplished something big, like running a marathon, curing a disease, or … making me feel something for him.

"We weren't misbehaving, Ma! Weston and I were discussing business. Some things we'd like to see over at Westy's. Everyone is putting in these virtual reality things, and I thought we might do something similar. I think it would be an amazing investment." Wes kept his arms around Kristy, hugging her tight. Her nose stayed crinkled.

I wondered what her real story was. She seemed harmless enough, but still, I was here for a job, and I needed to do my duty for Weston.

"Virtual reality? That's interesting. Have you been to Westy's, Kristy? What do you think?" I asked.

"Oh! Me? I, um … I don't get involved in such business matters. All I want to do is cook and clean and take care of kids! That other stuff is men's work." Kristy cringed, wiggling out of Wes's arms.

I bit my tongue, my lip, and held back my raging feminist soul, furiously rolling out the pie dough instead of saying my piece.

"Horseshit!" Ma said.

"Ma!" Weston cried.

"Well, it's true. Listen up here, Kristy. And you too, Nikki. Do you think I got all this by popping out babies and cleaning all the time? No! I love homemaking. Always have, always will. But I busted my rear end, getting our business off the ground. Wanna know who started the diner? Me. Wanna know who rolled that investment into the hotel? Me. The park was both my and Westy's project, but the majority of our assets and investments were strung together by yours truly. I am the backbone of the business. That might be Westy's name up there on the signs, but that was only a business decision too—by me. Westworld is Jeanworld—built for her family." Ma brushed the flour off her palms and began assembling the pie.

Wes and Weston looked at each other as if their mom had just performed the most significant mic drop in their history.

"It takes a damn strong woman to do that while raising these two. I want to be you when I grow up," I said, genuinely meaning it. My heart grew for Ma in that short speech. I'd liked her well enough before, but now, I admired her.

"You've no idea!" She huffed. "Now, get cleaned up and find some jobs to do. I'm finishing up in here and then getting myself ready for the guests."

Wes and Kristy whispered to each other as they left the kitchen.

"I'll meet you upstairs in a second, Weston." I shooed him away.

His eyes were still wide in shock from his mom's truth bomb. He slowly backed away. Once everyone left, I tried to comfort Ma. I couldn't help it. My conscience wouldn't let me leave the Banks' house without it after hearing the frustration in Ma's voice.

"I meant that, Ma. Women like you are who I look up to.

"My ma wasn't around much. She passed away from breast cancer when I was younger. You might have noticed that I avoided the topic of my family at dinner last night as best I could. It's still hard to talk about. But I think if I had a mother like you, I'd be able to conquer the world.

"You've been working your butt off in the shadows. I know how that feels. But I want you to know that I see your work, and I value it—all of the business and parenting. You made something special with all of it— especially Weston. Whatever you did to give him that big heart of his, the world needed that. And still needs more of it. For you to raise someone like that while juggling all of your businesses, you're my hero." I wiped my hands clean on a dish towel before throwing them around Ma and giving her the big hug I sensed she needed.

"Thank you, darlin'. I'm not sure what got into me just then. I guess it's the stress of the party. I wasn't always this way, ya know. With the homemaking." She sniffled. "I was career-driven. A different person back then. Sometimes, I do feel guilty, looking back and thinking of some of the times I missed the boys' childhood because I was helping get our businesses off the ground. And then, other times, I feel worthless and not taken seriously because all of what everyone, including my sons, saw was me changing diapers and baking these damn pies—not the countless hours building the park, the hotel, or the diner. Those accomplishments always went to their dad. I don't want you to think I don't love what I do. I just miss who I once was. Had to put that part of me aside. I guess I shouldn't have spouted off like that on poor Kristy!" She covered her mouth with her hand.

"Jean! Stop with the mom guilt. Weston thinks you're the greatest woman ever to live—and frankly, right now, I do too! Don't worry about Kristy. I bet she feels the same way. I haven't met many women who wouldn't. You deserve something for yourself too. I'm glad you let Jean out. It makes you more relatable."

"Yes, let Jean out. I did that, didn't I? Ha! Damn party stress is getting to me. If I were a drinker, I'd pour myself a whiskey right about now." She shook her head. "And you're very kind, Nikki. So glad my boy picked you. You remind me a bit of myself when I was younger, though I might have had a slight edge and a wild side to me." Her eyes glazed over.

*Oh, lady, if you only knew!*

"Now, that is something I'd like to hear about, too, one day. You just keep getting more and more interesting! I'm going to check on Weston and see if he needs my help with the fireworks stuff. He mentioned helping set it up earlier. Anything else I can do before I go?"

"No, dear. You've done more than you can imagine. Thank you," Ma said, wiping a tear from her eye before she thought I noticed.

# EIGHT

Weston

"I had no idea she felt that way." I sat on the edge of the bed and put my head in my hands. "I don't remember her working so much. I only remember her doing the mom stuff. Baking cow patties and shit."

"That's okay! I bet your dad doesn't know she feels that way either. Men can be oblivious to so much. That's what you got me for. I'm going to open your eyes a little bit, Weston. I think that's why I'm here. To teach you a lesson." Nikki rubbed her palms over my shoulders in a circular motion.

I closed my eyes and melted back into her hands.

"Does this lesson involve whips and chains?" I perked up.

"What the hell?"

"Well, you said we needed to get closer earlier. You wanted to shower with me even! Do I get a rain check on that?"

Nikki thumped Dan and stood up beside me. "Kiss me."

"Really? Okay. Is this how it all begins? You like a lot of foreplay?"

"If you don't shut your mouth and just kiss me, gah!"

I hopped to my feet, took the back of her head into my giant hand, and pushed her lips into mine. She slightly opened her mouth and traced my bottom lip with her tongue. My entire body became rigid. Her hand reached up, stroking the side of my face with her palm and letting her fingers trail all the way down Dan before bringing her lips to mine again. My dick stirred, and I might have let out a whimper as she gently stuck her tongue back into my mouth. I relaxed my shoulders and slowly slid my tongue into her mouth. My arm circled her waist as I pulled her into my hips and against my rock-hard cock. I pushed my mouth into her lips, harder, greedy for her breaths.

She pulled back, gasping for air. "Wow! That … you … Weston Banks. Where did you learn to kiss like that? You've been hiding that from me all along?"

"I feel … close to you. And when I feel close to someone, I turn on my smooth moves." I winked.

"Close to me, eh? Your fake fiancée. Good. I'm feeling close to you too." Her eyes darted toward the exit.

"Oh, yeah?" I asked, coming in for another kiss.

"Yeah," she muttered into my mouth.

I pulled back, out of breath and ready to take her to the next level.

"My tongue isn't only good for kissing. I'd love to twirl it around that clit of yours. I bet your pussy tastes like candy … or cream pies."

"Oh. Wow. Why don't you tell me how you really feel?" Nikki's eyes bulged.

"Fuck it. I will." I scooped her up into my arms and tossed her back onto the bed.

"Weston!" She feigned shock. "Did you at least lock the door?"

I turned to lock the door quicker than I'd ever done anything in my life. With one stealth motion, the door was locked, and I was on top of my fake bride.

"This is how I feel. I like you, and I've wanted to do this since I saw you dance on that stage. You said you wanted to get closer in the shower. This is a better idea." I kissed my way down her chest, circling her navel with my lips before lifting her dress.

She arched her back and moaned, not saying a word. I took her silence as a green light.

I slid my finger under her panties and tugged, gently kissing her skin. I nipped, nibbled, and caressed the skin just above her slit, making her buck against my face. I wanted her to beg for it. I needed her to beg—

"Knock, knock!" Ma called from outside the door.

My dick shriveled back into hiding.

Nikki's fist clenched the bedsheets. "Fuck!"

"It's okay. Another time," I growled, pushing myself off the bed. I unlocked the door and stepped out before shutting it and hoping she hadn't noticed Nikki in the bed.

"Your dad needs help with something or other out there. I think it's the fireworks station. Anyway, he asked me to get you," Ma said.

I nodded and followed her down the stairs, giving up on ever getting laid by the famous Crystal Cream Pie. Already, our fake engagement was coming to an end soon, and I'd not once gotten to fuck my fiancée.

I spent the next several hours with my dad and the vendors working at our event. While I sweated my itchy balls off, my brother was never even in sight. I loaded chairs into the back of my dad's pickup truck and slammed it shut.

"Hey, Dad, did you know Ma is more than just a ma?" I asked.

"What do you mean, son?" My dad climbed into the pickup and started the engine. It roared to life.

I always knew my father was home when our walls vibrated with his exhaust. All of the Banks men had a thing for cars.

"I guess she wasn't feeling valued or something. I don't know. She spouted off today about how she had built the business and stuff."

"She's absolutely right. I couldn't have done any of this without your mama. What set her off?"

"Kristy said business stuff was men's work."

"Phew, boy! Did she now? Ha-ha!" Dad slapped his knees. "Your mom might look like a '50s-era housewife, but that's because she plays that part well. She has a side she's hidden from you boys. Always told me she had to be in mom mode around y'all. Men's work … I can't believe she said that!" He laughed, rubbing his hand across his face.

"So, Ma's life doesn't revolve around Wes and me and you."

"Oh no, it does. It always has and always will. She's a special one. Balances it all. It's gotten to her a few times throughout the years. I have to dial up my work when that happens. But that's Jean. She would never call business men's work, no matter that she was always behind the scenes. She did most of the business stuff, to be honest with you. While I was out and about, getting financial resources, she was building it up."

"Why didn't I ever know this? I feel like my whole life has been a lie. I've had an amazing life. I've learned that now. But I don't want it at the expense of Ma's sanity."

"She gave up a big part of herself to be a mom. But you never knew that, did ya? She loves you. Just don't discount her work. I bet Kristy learned that quick. Besides, that ain't going nowhere. I'm not even sure Kristy is Wes's real fiancée."

I swallowed hard and stared out the window. "What makes you say that?"

"She just seems fake, is all. But your woman—that Nikki is something else! Reminds me of your ma when she was that age."

"Really? You think so? She's been good for me, and I love her so much," I said, feeling a knot in the pit of my stomach. It was halfway true. I hadn't been in love in ages, but I was falling for Nikki—and fast.

"You make a fine couple. Good enough to carry on the Banks name, I do believe. And you know, I'm looking to retire soon. Hoped to get one of my two buffoon sons to carry on with things. You seem like the more likely of the two to have a good head on your shoulders. What do you say?"

I blinked, slowly going over his words in my head and making sure I'd heard them right.

"Are you asking if I want to be the new big man in charge of Westworld?"

"Your brother is going to have a fit, but where is he now? He doesn't show up and work as you do. And Ma has high hopes for those grandbabies. Told me last night she can't wait for the wedding. Didn't know why y'all was keeping the date a secret. You might want to tell her that. I'll get with my lawyer and see what needs to be done when I do hand it over. That is, if you accept."

The guilt that fell on my shoulders weighed them down so much that they sagged heavy below my ears.

"I would love to take over Westworld." I gritted my teeth. Somehow, I'd thought I would feel better in this moment than I did.

I went about the rest of my day, making myself busy so as not to revel in the guilt I felt over my ma and dad believing I was marrying Nikki. I'd never thought about the repercussions of my decision. I wasn't one to look ahead into the future, but this time, I'd not been prepared at all. I wanted to confess to everyone that I was a lying dirtbag, but I didn't wish to drag Nikki into my drama. She didn't deserve it.

I watched her as she helped my ma set out her pies and adjust the table settings. Both Nikki and Ma laughed and danced around to the band warming up, and Ma even introduced her to the guests rolling in. Meanwhile, Kristy and Wes were attached to my dad at the hip. From Ma's rant earlier, I now knew that my mother was the one to win over in this business deal. She was the backbone. Wes was so oblivious to anyone but himself that he couldn't see that.

While he and his bullshit fiancée schmoozed my dad, Nikki had already won over my ma. But I knew by that look on her face that she wasn't even pretending anymore. Her wide smile and genuine laughter let me know that she was enjoying herself.

I grabbed a glass of sweet tea from the catering table and sat down at a table in the corner of the tent, drowning my guilt in a sugary drink that wasn't doing the trick. I needed a Shizzle Sauce cocktail now more than ever.

"I love her. I really, really love her, Weston. You did good, my boy," Ma whispered, setting a plate of food down in front of me.

"Oh, hey, Ma! I was watching you both earlier. It seems like you two were hitting it off. That's great!" My voice trailed off.

"She is something else; that's for sure! The total package. I'm going to want that wedding date before you leave the farm. I've got some stuff up my sleeve for it. Oh, and did your dad talk with you yet? About Westworld?"

I swallowed a lump in my throat. "He did. Asked if I was ready to take it on."

"And are you?"

"Yes, ma'am."

"Good! You know your father and I will still be working with you on it too. Don't stress out about it. We believe in you and know you'd not let us down." She patted my shoulder before heading back off toward the guests.

I pushed the food around on my plate before giving up on eating and settling back into my chair, fanning myself. The outdoor air conditioners placed around the tent weren't doing jack shit for my body. My blood pressure had skyrocketed through the roof by the time Nikki sat down next to me.

"Hey, stranger! Where have you been hiding? Left your bride all by her lonesome!" Nikki scooted her chair next to mine and swiped an olive from my plate.

"I got the offer. My dad told me I could have Westworld." I sighed.

"That's wonderful news!" Nikki grabbed the sides of my face and pulled me in for a big smack on the lips. "That means, our plan worked!"

"Yep."

"What's wrong?"

"They love you. Everyone loves you. I didn't think this through. I'm going to break their hearts. Especially Ma's. She is head over heels for you."

"I'm head over heels for her too. She is an amazing woman. I don't want to let her down either. I ... like her. Sure do wish my mom had been as caring and loving as she is! Whoever you marry will be lucky to have her as a mother-in-law. I thought, when I came here, she would be stiff and uptight, and she is, but your mama has a side to her that she's slowly been able to let out."

"I think it's because of you. I've never seen her like this. Look at her." I nodded toward my mom, who tossed her head backward, laughing with the band setting up onstage.

"How so?"

"I don't know. I guess you make her comfortable enough to tell her secrets. I knew she wasn't a Stepford mom ever since I found those dragon dildos. But I had no idea she was Jean—as horrible as that sounds. I never looked at my mom other than a mom. I'm an ass."

"You're not an ass. You're opening your eyes. No one has ever helped you see that, and you've been in a damn bubble—a comfy, cozy bubble where all is right in family and life. I get it. I would have been there too. But I've seen some shit, and I was forced to expand my views. I'm a better person for it, and maybe that is my path in life. Opening everyone's eyes. Spreading kindness and awareness around so others can pass on help where needed."

"You're amazing at that. I've been thinking about it. I think I'd like you to take me to the cottage sometime. I want to volunteer. Maybe even take some of the kids out here to the farm and show them how it all works. I think Ma would love it too."

"Really?" Her eyes lit up.

"Really." I smiled.

She scooted next to me and rested her head on my shoulder.

"This is the life," she sighed as we watched the guests laughing and enjoying themselves around us.

I nodded, kissing her hairline as she melted into me. She felt like part of the family. I closed my eyes for a split second, willing it so.

"Look at you two lovebirds!" Wes sneered, pausing to stop at our table.

Kristy's eyes darted around the room before settling on Nikki.

"You know, I've been trying to put my finger on where I know you from. You look so familiar. I kept racking my brain, trying to figure it out. But after that cream-pie comment in the kitchen, things just clicked. I've seen you at work, Crystal." Kristy smirked.

The hairs on the back of my neck bristled as my grip on Nikki tightened.

Nikki sat up, straightening her back. She stared into Kristy's eyes, causing Kristy to take a step back. "The Steamy Clam is my side job. Next time you're in there, you should stop and say hi."

"Oh, I don't go to those places." Kristy shivered. "I had a delivery there once. That was the first and last time I was in there."

"Is that so?" Nikki shifted in her chair. "Hmm. Delivery? I don't believe I ever even asked you what you do."

"I work for Pepe's." She grinned.

"Pepe's?" I asked.

"Yes, Pepe's. The taco place with the most amazing tacos ever!" Wes said, eyeballing Nikki.

"The taco place! Oh! I thought it was called Pee-Pee's. Certainly should be. Those tacos don't have shit on The Pink Taco Truck. Just saying." I shrugged my shoulders.

"Pee-Pee's!" Nikki laughed. "I love it. They are some pretty good tacos! But I have to admit, I'm partial to The Pink Taco Truck!"

"Of course. Those women do seem more … your type." Kristy's nose crinkled.

Nikki started to rise in her seat, but I gripped her tighter, holding her down.

"I'm sorry, what was that? What do you mean, those women are my type? Have you met any of those women?" Nikki's nose flared.

"No, and I don't want to. I've seen them. All tattoos, loud, mouthy, obnoxious. Dirty." Kristy tilted her head to the side and tapped her finger to her chin, as if trying to think of more ways to insult my fake bride.

"Wow, Wes! You sure did pick a bitch to settle down with. Let me guess. Is it that dying hyena laugh that won you over or the icy-cold cunt?" Nikki said, standing up. I couldn't keep her down any longer.

I rose to my feet behind her.

"Whoa! Control your woman, Weston." Wes stepped back, pulling Kristy with him.

"Control? Control?" Nikki laughed a laugh that I'd only heard in the movies by a supervillain.

My asshole clenched as I looked from my brother and his fiancée to Nikki and back. I was prepared to jump in, but at this point, I wasn't sure if Nikki would like that. I had a feeling she wanted to handle things herself. I put my palm on her lower back, only letting her know I was here, behind her all the way.

"Come on, Wes. It's not worth it. The deal will be off once your ma finds out her precious, future daughter-in-law is a stripper anyway." Kristy smiled, tugging Wes away before we could respond.

"He knows. He knows I've got Westworld, and he is building his case," I said, putting my arms around Nikki. Her body shook. "Are you okay? I'm so sorry you had to deal with that."

"I'm okay. I didn't want to make a scene, but damn, I wanted to knock that bitch out. How dare she talk about DTF! I mean, fuck. We are dirty but not dirty as in disgusting. Who the hell does she think she is?"

"She looks familiar to me, but she's a nobody. That's who. And she works at Pee-Pee's tacos. That says more of her than anything. Those tacos are nasty!"

"I'm sorry, Weston. I don't know how to do damage control on this one. I'll do my best. Who I am ... what I do ... that might ruin your chances of getting Westworld now. I don't think your ma will be thrilled about my secret life. Maybe we can tie it in with the breakup or something. Like I lied to you. Just blame it on me. All of it. I'm so damn sorry." She sat back down in her chair and folded her arms across her chest.

I plopped down beside her, resting my hands on her knees. "Hey. Don't be sorry. If things don't work out, it wasn't meant to be."

"But this is what I'm here for. I'm here to help you get what you want. This was a business deal, remember? I failed on my part."

"No, you didn't. I got Westworld. They must know it, and they're probably grasping at straws to change my parents' minds. We'll figure it out. And even if we don't, I'm glad I made this business deal with you. Like we talked about earlier, you've opened my eyes. I already feel like a better man because of you. Also, you're hot as fuck, and I got to stick my tongue in your mouth. It's still a winning situation for me, no matter the outcome."

"You're one in a million, Weston—and Dan," she said, tugging at my beard and pulling me in for a kiss.

# NINE

*Nikki*

I crawled into bed, more mentally exhausted than anything. I hadn't even enjoyed the fireworks because of the guilt I felt for Weston and his family. Not only was I about to fail him at our business arrangement because of my reputation, but I would also hurt his mother, who, in the short amount of time I'd been here, I had grown close to. Weston and I hadn't discussed any more of the drama tonight. I wore my heart on my sleeve, and the sadness that fell on me like a heavy blanket carried over to him as well.

He had tried to cheer me up throughout the night, but my heart was already broken. I worried that I'd fucked up, and I was not the type of person who handled failure very well. I worked my ass off at my jobs. I wasn't even worried about the money and paying off my debts at this point. All I wanted was to see Weston and his family happy—and maybe for that bitch Kristy to be trampled by Bessie.

I twirled my mother's ring on my finger, whispering a quick prayer to whoever would listen, "Please help me figure out a way not to let Weston and his family down. Please help the DTF girls. Please help the cottage children. Please save the world. Amen."

I pulled the blankets up around my neck and curled up on my side.

The door slowly creaked open.

"Nikki?" Weston called.

"Weston? I thought I'd locked that door!" I whispered back.

"You did. I'm sorry. I picked it."

"You can pick locks?"

"Yes."

"Hmm. That's a little out of character, but I think I like it," I called out into the dark, my eyes adjusting to him as he quietly shut the door.

"Can we talk?"

"Sure. Come on in." I threw back the covers and let him slide in next to me. "I'm assuming this is the damage control talk. You know … I was thinking—" I started.

Weston pressed his lips into mine and crawled on top, straddling me. Dan brushed against my chin, sending tingles—really, really good tingles—down my body and out my toes.

"Shh … I need to know my wife."

"Fiancée," I breathed out and into his lips. He tasted like whiskey. "Weston! Do you have alcohol you aren't sharing?" I sat up on my elbows as he leaned back and took a flask from his pajama pocket.

"I needed a drink tonight. It's my dad's flask. I have known where he hides it since I was a boy."

He unscrewed the cap and handed it to me. I took a long, slow swig and let the fiery heat wash over me.

"That is some good stuff." I groaned, taking an even bigger swig before handing it back to him. "Now, where were we? Oh, yes. You need to get to know your wife."

"Fiancée," he said, taking a sip of the flask and leaning over to set it on the nightstand.

I could barely see his body in the dark room, but I felt the bed jostling enough to know that he was undressing.

He swung his leg around and wiggled out of his onesie. "Too bad these damn things don't have a front flap. Would make this easier."

"For you." I grinned. "I'm going to stay in my warm pajamas and just ..." I rolled over on my stomach and reached behind me, unbuttoning the flap covering my ass.

"Fuck," he said as I pushed my ass into the air.

"Shh! It's bad luck to fuck before the wedding. Your ma might here!"

"Oh, please don't mention her when I'm staring at the most delicious thing in the world."

He leaned down and bit my left ass cheek hard, causing me to gasp. He pulled my hips up and into his face, licking every inch of me from behind. My clit throbbed hard with each flick of his tongue before he slid it straight into my dripping pussy. I bit the corner of my pillow.

*Damn! Goofball Weston has a wild side in him too.*

My inner thighs were already soaked when he paused and ripped open a condom before quickly returning to my bare ass in the air.

*He came in here, prepared for this! That little weasel!*

I grinned into my pillow as I felt his cock rub against my ass. "Warmer," I whispered as he slid himself through the opening of my pajamas and all the way down my slit. "Much, much warmer."

He teased my pussy, barely sticking the tip of his cock inside.

"Hot!" he groaned, pushing himself in deep and rough. Really, really rough.

My hands slid out in front of me and gripped the bedsheets as his thick cock stretched me out so much that I'd have a hard time walking tomorrow.

"You like that, don't ya?" I egged him on, wincing with a good pain each time his dick hit my cervix. I pushed my hips back into him, wanting more.

"You have no idea," he muttered, rising to his feet and squatting behind me while still keeping his dick inside.

He leaned over me, placing his palms under my chin and tilting my head back as he slammed into me. His thumbs slipped inside my mouth. I bit down on them to keep from groaning.

This was a move even I'd never done before. Sure, I had fucked from the back plenty, but not with a man jabbing me from behind while maintaining his balance on his feet. I had no idea how this giant man was doing it, but he sure as hell was doing it and doing it so damn well.

"Fuck, fuck, fuck!" I groaned as we bounced on the bed. My hand slipped under my waist as I circled my clit through my onesie.

"Shh ..." He covered my mouth with one of his hands and left the other tilting my neck back.

He slowed his pace, slamming into me harder. My cervix would ache tomorrow, but I loved that. I wanted to feel my man the next day and relive these steamy moments.

"You're giving it to me so damn good, Weston. I love the way your big cock feels inside me. Don't stop. Please. Don't stop. I need it." I bucked my hips against him harder, trying to make up for his slower pace. I wanted it fast and hard. I needed it fast and hard.

"Whoa, whoa, whoa. I can't ... I—"

"Give it to me, baby! I'm going to pull that hot cum out of you. It's mine. Oh! Weston, Weston, Weston ..." I moaned his name as he covered my lips with his palm again and grunted, burying himself inside of me.

My body convulsed, my hips wiggled, and I bit his palm until I tasted blood. I came harder than I'd ever come in my entire life. I throbbed on his cock as he let go of my neck and cried out, gripping my hips and pulling me into him. I looked behind me just as his knees began to wobble, and he fell over. His cock stuck straight into the air with the condom barely hanging on. It looked like a white flag of surrender.

I rolled over onto my back, unable to catch my breath. Weston was breathing like he had just run a marathon or like we'd fucked like rabbits, which we had. And it was damn amazing.

"I have no idea where you learned all that, but you blew my mind, Weston," I said between breaths.

"It was that dirty talk you did. That sent me into overdrive! I love that filthy mouth of yours. Please feel free to talk to me like that anytime." He sat up on the bed. "Be right back. Let me, erm … clean up."

"You're going out there, naked?"

"I'll be quiet and back in no time."

It was less than a minute before he was back between the sheets with me.

"It seems like you've had to do that before. Sneaking around and all," I whispered as he spooned into me.

"Maybe a few times … as a teen. Never as a grown man. That whole secrecy and being quiet though certainly adds to a new level of sexiness. I thought sex with you would be exciting, but between having to be quiet and your dirty talk, I was mind-blown. How was it for you? What you expected?"

"Much, much more than I'd expected. You surprised me. For some reason, I'd thought you'd be more … innocent in bed. More vanilla. Maybe just missionary for the first few times."

He gasped, pulling me back into him tight and nibbling my ear. "I'm more reserved outside of the bedroom, but I do have handcuffs and a blindfold in my closet. Maybe, you know, if you ever want to swing by my place, me and my boy Dan can show you the ropes. Literally. I have those too. Four-poster bed and all. That is, if you like that sort of thing."

"Wait a minute." I switched to my other side, facing him. "You are into BDSM? You like to tie chicks up? Are you into dominating?"

He stroked the hair from my face, pausing to lean down and kiss me. "Only if you're comfortable with it. It's not something I have a lot of experience with, but when I have done it, I've enjoyed it. But … don't let that scare you off. I—"

"Fuck yeah! I love that shit! Wow. Weston Banks has a closet full of ropes and goodies. Do you have a ball and a gag? That is something I've not tried, but I desperately want to!" I clasped my hands under my chin, suddenly more attracted to this giant goofball than I'd ever been.

"Nope, but I'm sure I can get one off Amazon in a day or two. Consider it on the way." He kissed my forehead and smiled.

"I'm down. As long as you still want to see me once the shit hits the fan with Wes and Kristy. Do you think I should just go in the morning? Sneak out and miss it all? What do you want to do?" I asked.

"I want to fall asleep beside you and not worry about any of it until the morning."

"First of all, your mom will wake up early and catch us. Second of all, you have to be prepared!"

"I am prepared. I love you as my fiancée, no matter your job or whatever you do. Does that bother you though? People knowing you're a stripper?"

"Hell no. I don't give a damn about my reputation. All I care about is surviving a happy and peaceful life and spreading that positive energy shit into the world. I just don't want our lie and my life to screw yours up."

"Nothing—absolutely nothing—about you is going to fuck my life up. I'm not that type of fake husband. I'm proud to have my fake wife by my side. As for the other, you can set your alarm for four. I'll sneak back out then. We will be good. Remember, I've done it all before." He rubbed my shoulder and leaned forward to kiss the tip of my nose.

"Fiancée," I whispered, reaching for my phone and setting the alarm.

"Oh, right. Fiancée. Fake fiancée. We're not married yet." He sighed.

I bopped Dan before resting my head on Weston's chest and falling asleep.

"Rise and shine!" Ma's voice called from the bottom of the stairs.

"Shit! Did the alarm not go off?" I whispered to Weston, who was sleeping facedown into a pillow. I rolled him over. "Hey! How can you even breathe like that? Get up! Your mom is here!" I shook him awake.

"What? Huh?" Weston groaned.

"Breakfast is on the table! It's getting cold. I'm not walking up them stairs this morning after my partying last night! Git down here!" Ma yelled.

"Shit! She's up. What time is it?" He rubbed his eyes.

"Seven!" I said, checking my phone.

"I guess I wore us out last night. Was I dreaming, or did you and I do it four times?"

"Not a dream. Very much real. You kept waking up and nudging me, and, well, I couldn't resist. I'm not sure I can walk this morning, but we've got to get down to breakfast and do any damage control that might come up. Remember, your stripper fiancée?"

"Fuck my brother and Kristy," Weston said, rolling off the bed. "I have some information up my sleeve if they decide to pull any crap."

"Oh, really? Okay. Hopefully, you won't need to use it. Just be careful, Weston. Don't play with fire. You want this. This is your life goal. Come on, don't give up now." I slowly pulled myself off the bed. The ache in my thighs made me cringe as I hobbled to the dresser mirror and checked that I didn't have any bite marks on my neck. "Eyes on the prize, buster!" I glanced back at him before heading downstairs, clutching the rail with each step.

Weston followed behind me, wincing with each step he took too.

"What's the matter?" I giggled. "Too many squats on your leg day? Feeling that muscle soreness?"

"Never. I don't tire out. I'm a machine," he said, his voice shaking just as much as his legs.

"Sure, sure. Weston Banks, the machine."

I hooked my arm around him, shuffling into the kitchen. Weston's brother and Kristy were already seated.

"Look who finally decided to join us! My dearest brother and his super sweet fiancée. They are just the most darling, innocent-looking couple. Wouldn't you say so, Kristy?" Wes smiled as I gently lowered myself into the chair.

"They make a beautiful couple. Now, eat your food." Ma's voice was harsh. She walked back to the kitchen counter.

"Can I help with anything?" I asked, lifting myself back up to do anything I could for her. "Are you okay? You look like your feet hurt."

"No, no. I'm fine. About to sit down myself. My feet are just sore from last night's dancing, is all. I haven't danced like that in a long time."

"Dancing?" Kristy asked. "I must have been so busy eating all that good food that I didn't see you out there on that dance floor! I bet Nikki here did though. She loves dancing. Did you show her any of your moves?"

The grin that played across her lips made my stomach tighten. Mean girls. That was what she was. She was playing the game too, trying to help out Wes. There was no way she was his girlfriend. I could see it in their body language. She couldn't stand him. I wondered how much he was paying her and if she genuinely worked at Pee-Pee's. She had told me that bullshit story of how'd they met after helping that old lady across the street, but something was fishy, and two could play her blackmail game.

"I didn't have a chance to show her. But I'm sure she has her signature moves. She doesn't need my input. What about you? How did you guys like the band? Planning on hiring one for your wedding? I'd love to talk about weddings with you! Tell me about what y'all are planning." I stretched a napkin across my lap and reached across the table, grabbing one of Ma's famous cinnamon rolls.

"Yes, let's hear about this wedding!" Ma agreed. "Both of them!"

"Like how much they're going to cost," Westy muttered.

"Hush you! You only get married once. Well, in our family. You choose the right one and make it work. Isn't that right, honey?" Ma leaned over and patted Westy's shoulder.

"Yes, dear," he answered. "And that is lesson one in husbandry: always respond, *Yes, dear*, and things will be fine."

"I don't think that word means what you think it means, Westy, but that's beside the point." Ma shook her head.

"Husbandry? What else would you call it? I've heard that word before somewhere," Westy continued.

"Never mind, you. It's not being a husband. Lord help us." Ma blew out a breath. "You two, spill the beans on the weddings. I've got some ideas in mind too. It's my boys' only wedding, and I don't want to be a meddling mother-in-law, but there are some traditions I'd love to see them follow. So, go."

Kristy looked back and forth from Wes to Ma. "You go first, Nikki!" she spit out.

"I'd love to. Well, Jean, I know we've been secretive about the wedding date, but we weren't sure how you'd feel about it, so we were hesitant to say anything. However, after getting to know you more, Weston and I are excited to say that we want to get married on your anniversary. We know it's a little ways away since y'all just celebrated, but will you let us share your special day with you?" I scooted my chair next to Weston, who was either genuinely smiling or had the best poker face I'd ever seen.

"Oh my word! Yes! That is the sweetest, isn't it, Westy?" Ma clasped her hands under her chin and grinned. "You two following in our footsteps. I'm sure it's because Weston told you we did the same with his parents? That date has been in the family for generations."

"That is exactly why I wanted to grab it first!" Weston said, smiling at his brother.

I had no clue how that little lie had come together perfectly, but I gripped my crystal necklace and said a mental prayer to whoever was watching out for us.

"What else can you tell me?" Ma beamed at me.

"We'd like to get married here, on the farm. I know how much work it is to throw a party, and I don't want you to worry about a thing! We would have that all taken care of," I said, staring at Weston instead of Ma. I hoped my gaze silently communicated that I needed his help in this.

"Yep. We'll hire the caterers, cleaning crew, and all that. We'd like it out by the creek if possible. I've been thinking about building one of those arbors to overlook that area and make it nice. Hoped Dad could help with that." Weston scooted his chair closer to me and threw his arm around my shoulders.

"That sounds perfect!" Ma bounced in her chair.

"Yep, sounds *so* perfect. That's my brother—always perfect," Wes sneered.

"Is that jealousy I sense, Wes? You know I love you and think you are perfect too! Tell me about your wedding plans." Ma leaned forward in her chair, waiting on Weston's brother to answer.

"Well, we originally planned on your wedding date too. But I guess that's taken now," Kristy said. Her lip downturned into a pout.

"Nonsense! You can always have a double wedding. Only if that is okay with the brides. Maybe y'all will have babies at the same time, too, and I can have more grandbabies to love!" Ma said.

"I don't mind sharing!" I said. "The more, the merrier! I'm sure Kristy and I would get along just fine."

"Of course." Kristy blinked.

"Perfect. Hey! You never told Weston the story of how y'all met. Can you tell it again? It's super sweet," I said, crossing my legs and leaning back in my chair.

Kristy's cheeks flushed pink. "Oh, you know. A typical day, helping an old lady across the street. That's not very interesting. What about you? Did you meet Weston where you work? Where is it do you work again?"

"She works at a restaurant, don't ya, love?" Ma patted my knee.

"Oh, right. Do you serve clams? Hot and steamy ones." Kristy smiled at Wes, who grinned right back at her.

Weston's jaw muscle twitched as I watched his long, bony fingers slowly curl and uncurl into a fist. "I did meet her at work. She works for The Pink Taco Truck and also works as a dancer at The Steamy Clam. She also volunteers to help at-risk youth. She's the most wholehearted, exciting, caring, and gorgeous woman I've ever met, and I'm damn lucky to have her in my life."

My heart plummeted into my stomach. Weston had had to go and play hero and destroy his chances of Westworld—for me.

"The Steamy Clam?" Ma's brows pulled together as she looked from me to Weston. "You're a stripper?"

"I am on the side. My main job is with my best friends, working The Pink Taco Truck, but I dance on the side for extra cash. I fell on hard times and needed the cash to pay off some debts. Luckily, the staff at The Steamy Clam took me in and showed me the ropes. Weston has supported me fully one hundred percent in making my own independent choices to be who I am and get to where I need to be. It's me who is damn lucky to have him in my life," I said those last words carefully while staring straight into Weston's eyes. I saw Dan tremble slightly and knew Weston was about to tear up.

"Ma? Are you okay?" Weston said.

The silence that fell on the table was deafening.

"You're dating a stripper! Of course she's not okay!" Wes cried.

Weston stood up, knocking his chair back. "Do you have a problem with my fiancée? Because we can talk about yours and how she is some woman you met on a sugar-daddy website and how you're paying her to act like your fiancée. Her name isn't even Kristy. It's Kristen." He pointed his finger at his brother.

Kristy's eyes bulged. "You don't know what you're talking about. Kristy is short for Kristen!" she groaned.

"Oh, yeah? Check it out. Pulled straight from SugarDaddio-dot-com!" Weston pulled a piece of paper from his back pocket and unfolded it before throwing it on the table.

I raised my eyebrows. I wasn't going to touch that piece of paper. Weston's word was enough for me, and besides, I wasn't a drama llama.

Ma shook her head and slowly stood up. "I'm going to go lie down," she said, shuffling her feet out the door.

"But, Ma, wait!" Wes called after her.

"Leave her be, son. I'll speak to both of you in a bit. I think it's time you both pack up your things. Your ma and I need some time to think." Westy leaned his elbows on the table and rested his head in his hands.

"Come on, Weston. Let them have some time," I whispered, pulling Weston up the stairs.

Wes and Kristy followed behind us, bickering under their breaths.

"You know I would have never left you out to dry, asshole! No matter who Dad signed the papers over to! You would have always been part of my team! That's what family is for!" Weston turned toward his brother. "Now, look! We both are fucked!"

"Whatever, Weston. You were playing games, bringing her here. You and I are close enough to know that both of us were playing games!" Wes gritted his teeth.

"Mine is real. Nikki is no game for me," Weston said.

I put my arm around his waist and leaned into him. "You don't have to explain yourself. Let's just get out of here."

"I'm real too!" Kristy said, stomping her foot.

"No, no. You're not. You're not even my type. Show's over. I'm taking your ass home. Couldn't you have at least been more damn discreet online? What the hell?" Wes shook his head before disappearing down the hall.

Weston and I quickly gathered our things and crept downstairs to an empty kitchen. A scribbled note lay on the table, reading, *Love you both. We will discuss this another day.*

"We can't leave without saying good-bye!" Weston cried, pacing back and forth in the entry. "I always hug and kiss my ma and dad before saying good-bye! What if something happens to them, and this is the last time I got to see them?"

"You're going to have to respect their wishes and give them the space they want. The note said they want to discuss it all another day, so you're just going to have to let them have some time. I'm so sorry, Weston," I said, rubbing his back and gently pushing him out the door and into the P-wagon.

My time as a new member of the Banks family was over.

# TEN

Weston

My mood was so blown to shit that I didn't even turn the hydraulics on in the pussy wagon when we left the farm. I'd had everything in my grasp, and yet it'd slipped through my fingers. All of it—even the only part I cared about these days.

"How did you know about Kristy?" Nikki asked on the drive home.

"I looked at the site too. Like brother, like brother, I guess. Or something like that. Anyway, it's a site full of women who will pretty much do anything for money. I contemplated using it, but the ones I interviewed all seemed vicious and vile. I wasn't comfortable with being so cutthroat about my approach," I replied, clenching my jaw.

"Wow, I never knew such a thing existed. I guess we all need to make money somehow. I bet there are some really good ones on there who just need the help to make ends meet too."

"Yes, I bet you're right. You're always right. I don't open my eyes a lot, but you've helped with that. I appreciate it."

"Thank you. At least I could add a little positivity to the situation. I'm sorry, Weston. About all of it. I did my best. I just don't think a stripper is a good fit for you and your family. You're all very sweet and innocent, and I'm … I'm not. I've been through too much ever to be a robotic wife and turn a blind eye to the world while raising ten babies. You deserve a nice girl who is going to bake cow patties and shit," she said.

"You have always been miles beyond what I deserve. There's no one like you, Nikki. I'm the one who is sorry. I blew it. I should have just dated you properly and seen where it went instead of coming up with this stupid lie. It was dishonest and rather shitty of me to drag you into it. I hate that I hurt you and my ma." I pushed my foot down on the gas pedal. I needed this nightmare to be over before I told her how I felt—which was that I'd fallen for her. That night we had finally joined as fake man and fake fiancée was the best sex of my life. Not because she blew my mind and I blew my load, but also because I felt something more after that. When I had been getting deep into her, she had been getting deep into me.

"I'm so upset I disappointed your mother. I think I'll try to reach out to her in time and apologize, if that is okay with you. She was growing on me. Like a real mom." Nikki leaned her forehead into the window and sighed.

"And me too? You'll still reach out to me? Even though our whole charade is over? I'd still love to date you. The other night, that meant something to me."

*Stupid, Weston.*

"Step back for a minute. Think about what all you could have. I'm not that girl. I'm a taco-making stripper. I'll not be baking cookies and shit or popping out babies. I'm fulfilled in life with the kids from the cottage, and after a long day of making tacos, the last thing I would want to do is make cow patties. Give it some time. If you think it's what you want, you know where to find me. We can discuss it all then. I just think everyone needs time."

"Understood," I breathed out.

I felt like a knife had gone straight through my heart. Yet again, I had stuck my foot in my mouth. I told the truth and blew it all. If I had kept my lips sealed, we might not have been in this predicament now. I could possibly be getting road head, for crying out loud!

We drove the rest of the way to Nikki's apartment in a mixture of sad silence and '80s tunes. After today, I could get back to normal at my own quiet place. There would be no more shenanigans and no more lies. I'd need to apologize later on in the week and explain things to my parents, but for now, my only concern was wading through this fake breakup from my fake engagement.

"I'll send you a check, if that is okay," I said, pulling into the parking lot in front of Nikki's place and popping the trunk.

"You will do no such thing. I failed at this job. You might not have noticed this, but I don't take handouts. You've done plenty. Let me experience family life. I always wanted to do that. You're a lucky man, Weston." She leaned over the console and kissed my cheek. "And you too, Dan," she said, thumping my beard. "Don't be a stranger at The Steamy Clam. Next lap dance is on me!"

She twisted the fake engagement ring off her hand.

"Keep it," she whispered, pushing it into my palm.

My fingers curled around it, brushing against hers. "What am I going to do with it? I don't need it."

"You're going to give it to your real fiancée. Someone … deserving. Look, Weston. I can't apologize enough about the whole situation. I didn't mean to let it get this far. I'm so, so sorry. I never meant to hurt you or your family," she said, hopping out of the car.

"I'll keep it," I called after her. "But I'm still going to pay you. So, be expecting it. You don't do handouts, and I don't do breaking my word. You did the job. A damn good job too. And you, please don't be a stranger either. Come to Westy's sometime. I'll get you and your girls some annual passes."

"Now, annual passes to Westy's I can't pass up. But that will be enough. Thank you, Weston," she said, pulling her gigantic bag from the trunk.

"Let me help you!"

"No way. You know I got it. I can do it on my own."

"I know you can," I whispered as I watched her walk away and disappear into her apartment.

The following week, I threw myself into work. I marketed the Westworld brand to anyone and everyone who would listen. I signed a contract with a new pretzel vendor for Westy's, hired a few weirdos for our upcoming Halloween freak show, and hired a contractor to draw up some renovation ideas for the hotel so that I could at least pitch my thoughts to my dad.

I hadn't seen or heard from my parents since Nikki, and I had left a week ago. I also hadn't heard from Nikki.

I wanted to give her the space she'd asked for, but I was only doing it for her. I didn't need the space. I knew exactly what I wanted. Sure, having a trophy wife at home, making my meals and cleaning my house, sounded pretty damn good to me. But I already had a housekeeper, and I enjoyed dining out. I wanted a partner in life.

My mind kept drifting back to the night Nikki and I'd banged. The way she'd felt when I slid inside of her reminded me of a hot, buttered biscuit—or pie. Cream pie. Fuck, I wanted to give her a cream pie, and now, I'd not have the chance.

I slid my phone out of my pocket and hovered my finger over her name in my Contacts list but ultimately chickened out. Instead, I hopped into my P-wagon and drove to Frannie, the fortune teller.

If anyone had any insight into Nikki, it had to be her. I contemplated contacting her DTF friends, but I'd only met them once, and to be honest, they scared the shit out of me. Frannie was only a slightly safer choice, but she was all I had. Maybe she could give me information from their private talks that would help me be the man Nikki needed.

I hurried up the crumbling concrete steps and rang Frannie's doorbell just as she opened the door.

"I've been expecting you." Frannie smirked.

"Really? That's scary. Did you see me coming here in that big glass ball thing?" I asked.

"No, I did not see you in the crystal ball. I just knew you'd be here for advice once you and Nikki's lie backfired in your face. Doesn't take a fortune teller to know that wasn't going to work," she said, motioning for me to come inside.

"Well, why didn't you warn me?"

"I did! I said, be careful and tread lightly. I also told you that you had a chance, and you being back here alone makes me think you ruined it. Am I right?"

"I don't know. Everything just blew up. I told my parents about her work at the strip club. I thought I was doing the right thing by being honest and standing up for her. But I don't think she liked that."

"No, she did. I'm sure of that. What makes you think she didn't?"

"Really? She said she needed some space, and she didn't think a stripper was a good fit for my family and me."

Frannie snorted. "If she only knew."

"What was that?" I asked, tugging at Dan and searching the room for that damn black cat.

I felt his eyes on me. He was probably cursing me now.

"You shouldn't be here, talking to me. You should be talking to your parents. Have you spoken to them since the lie came out? Your fake engagement?"

"No. I'm too ashamed to talk to them."

"Oh, Weston, Weston, Weston. You've got a lot to learn." She pinched the bridge of her nose.

"Apparently. I've learned a lot over the last few weeks. Let's see. I'm privileged as hell, my mom has some resentment for mom life and was the backbone of Westworld, I can't trust my brother at all anymore, and there's such a thing as coochie cream. I feel like all I've been doing these last few weeks is learning." I ran my hand through my hair and sighed.

"You can't grow without learning. But there's still much to learn. That's why you're going straight to your parents' house from here. Call them and let them know you're coming. They have more to tell you. I think what they can do for you will help you get through those walls Nikki has built up around her. The key to Nikki isn't just you, but it's your parents too. Especially Ma. I'm betting they took a deep likening to one another."

"How did you know? I thought they were completely opposite and going to butt heads, but they seemed to get closer than even me and Nikki!"

"Anyone ever tell you that you have mommy issues? Everyone does this. I should have been a damn therapist. Y'all out there, picking folks who are just like your parents!" She shook her head before putting her hands on her hips. "Now, go talk to your ma!"

"What does that mean? Nikki and my ma are polar opposites!"

"Mmhmm. Go. Your answers aren't here. They are with your family. And your family will be the answer to Nikki. It will all come together. Just don't put that damn foot in your mouth, ya big goofus." Frannie stood on her tiptoes to kiss me on the cheek before shoving me back out the door.

I stumbled to my car, drunk on confusion. The thought of facing the firing squad, my parents, after my big, fat lie, had my legs shaking already. I dialed my ma's number to let her know I was coming.

I cringed as soon as she answered the phone. "Ma, I'm on my way. I need to talk to you."

"You finally decided to call us! If you ever disappear like that again, boy, I'll tan your hide! You know how frightening it is for a mother when she can't get in touch with her kid?" Ma's voice rose through the phone.

"I know. I'm sorry. Really, I am. I'll be there in a few minutes. Love you. See you." I hung the phone up, started my ignition, and crawled the pussy wagon all the way to the farm. I barely tapped my gas pedal, taking my time. This conversation wasn't one I wanted to have at all. I turned up the volume on my radio and tried to zone out, but my mind kept drifting back to Nikki.

By the time I pulled up at my parents' farm, I had already relived my entire weekend with her in my head. I thought about the way her legs had wrapped around me, how she'd wanted me to chase her in the mud, how her ass had looked in the air when she unbuttoned her pajamas. My dick grew thick in my pants, keeping me confined to my car. Bessie slowly waddled over to my rolled-down window.

"Moo," I said.

"Mooooooooooo," she called back.

"Really? Well, that's strange," I answered her as I waited for my cock to shrivel back up, which took no time at all because I was talking to a cow, who I was pretty sure had just told me that Ma was in a good mood. I didn't know how I knew this, but it just happened that way with Bessie. I made a mental note to ask Frannie about my ability to speak cow and just what the hell that meant.

*Why does it have to be a cow?* I wondered as I slammed the car door and slowly pulled myself up the front porch steps. *Why can't I talk lion? Or snake? Or shark?* I snickered to myself as I tried to make the noises that I thought sharks made, which sounded a lot like a whale. I probably could speak whale too.

"What the heck are you doing?" Ma asked from the porch swing.

"Ahh! You scared me! I didn't even see you sitting there." My heart plummeted into my stomach.

I had been so in my head that I didn't even notice my parents. That porch swing where they sat was the bane of my existence. I knew I was about to endure a serious conversation when my parents were outside on the porch, and if there was a pitcher of sweet tea, it was even worse. That meant that we would be here for a while. I glanced at the tea on the table beside the swing. No good conversations happened on the porch.

I swallowed hard, clenched my fists, and held my breath as I walked over to them.

"Son, sit down. We need to talk," Dad said, motioning me toward a chair.

I plopped myself down and wiped a bead of sweat from my brow. "It's about my giant screwup, isn't it? About Nikki. I should have told you the truth about what she did. She's not ashamed of it, and I shouldn't have been either. I knew it wasn't something y'all would go for but—"

"Weston! Can you shut that hairy trap of yours for a minute and listen to us? Your dad and I need to talk to you about something." Ma slapped her palm on her leg.

"Sheesh. I'm sorry. Okay. Go ahead." I scratched my head and clenched my butt, preparing myself to be kicked out of the Banks' will for good.

"Your dad and I didn't meet as high school sweethearts. We met at a club called Bottoms Up," Ma huffed.

"Okay." I shrugged my shoulders. "That some type of beer-drinking honky-tonk or something?"

"It's a strip club." Ma twisted her palms together before rubbing them down her muumuu.

"What?" I wasn't sure if I'd heard my mom correctly. She couldn't have said *strip club*.

My mom had been a waitress in high school and throughout college. She had been part of the choir and gone to church regularly. She would never set foot in a strip club—not my mom.

"I worked there—as a stripper. I was a stripper. Your dad was my best customer." She smiled at Dad before looking back at me and puffing up her chest.

My mouth hung open stupidly.

"You're telling me that I've been thinking we're the perfect '50s-style family with a mom who bakes and a dad who runs his own business when, in reality, my mom was a stripper?"

"We still are the perfect family! Heavens! I don't strip anymore. Look at these veins!" Ma stuck her leg out and pulled up her muumuu, showing me the throbbing snakes she called veins that ran down her legs.

"But why did you hide that then? Why weren't you ever real with Wes and me? It's the same thing as when you said you worked so much, building the business, and you got upset that you hadn't gotten credit. I feel like I don't even know my own mom! Or dad! Dad? What did you do to Mom? You were what, stuffing money down her drawers or something? This is just insane!" I pushed myself up from my chair and walked to the other side of the porch. I had to look somewhere, anywhere, other than my parents' faces. I stared down at Bessie, who I could swear was laughing.

*Fucking cow-speak curse.*

"Because we are from a different era. What I used to do wasn't widely accepted, if at all back then. I wanted my boys to have a normal life. Once I married Westy, I was able to give up that life for good and put it behind me. Not that I had any issues with it. I didn't. I still don't. But for my children, I wanted to keep you safe. I didn't want you to be made fun of or have any problems arise in the community for you. So … we moved away just a bit and started fresh—me as a '50s housewife. Building the business gave me a little bit of the independence I craved but nothing like I needed. And now …" Ma tapped her fingers on the table.

"You're going to strip again?" I shouted, turning back toward them.

"Did you not just see my legs? Focus!" Ma groaned.

"Now that my children are grown, I feel like I can be me again. It's been an issue this last year or so. Hell, it's probably menopause. But your dad and I have been wanting to tell you and your brother this for a while. When we learned that sweet girl Nikki was working the same job I'd had, well, we figured it was a good time. We just didn't know how. So, here we are. Any questions?" Ma crossed her arms over her chest and leaned back in the swing.

"Why? Why did you need to strip? Was there anything wrong?"

"No. Why does there need to be something wrong? I liked dancing, and the money was good. That's all. I would still be doing it now if it wasn't for these here damn legs! I'm telling you!" She leaned forward and tapped both of her calves.

"Thank you for telling me, Ma. You've always been the best mother anyone could ask for. I don't yet know if I am happy that you spilled your secret life to me or if I'd rather not have known. But I am glad you feel comfortable enough with me to share. It just makes me rethink my childhood."

"Was it a bad childhood?" Dad asked.

"No," I answered quickly.

"Then, what does it matter?" Ma tilted her head and studied my face.

"I guess it doesn't."

"Good. Now, I have to explain things to my soon-to-be daughter-in-law, and this will all blow over. We can get back to it. Get your name on the papers, and then you can start supplying me grandbabies."

"Ma, we broke up. She didn't think she was good enough for me—or you. She felt bad and didn't want to ruin the Banks name. Said I deserve better. Also, she doesn't want kids. She has her hands full at the cottage with the disadvantaged youth. She loves those children as her own." I walked back over to my seat and sat down, rubbing my hands over my eyes.

"No kids? I thought y'all said you were interested?" Ma clutched her chest.

"She wanted to impress you. She wanted you to like her. Nikki is amazing, Ma. But she doesn't want kids, and she is a stripper. She's also pretty damn outspoken, she comes from a hard knock life, and she lights sage sticks on fire. Calls it smudging. It's supposed to get rid of bad energy or whatever," I said.

"The grandchildren talk can come later. Boy, get your ass back up to that Juicy Clam or whatever the hell it's called and get your woman. I'm telling you from experience, if she can work the pole, she can work the pole. She's a catch you don't want to get rid of!" Dad wagged his finger at me.

"Oh, gross, Dad! I thought sex before marriage was forbidden! Ma made sure Nikki and I had separate bedrooms! Just what kind of brothel are we running here these days?" I cried, getting back up and heading toward my car.

"I didn't say anything about sex, son. There are other ways, ya know. Damn, are you that dense?" Dad shook his head.

"Stop! Just stop!" I put both of my hands in the air. "Point taken. I'm out. I'll talk to Nikki or figure out something. Maybe get her back here for y'all both to explain yourselves. Just no more talk of this dirty stuff, please."

"Deal. If you hear from Wes, please don't tell him. We are going to speak to him privately too. Let me know something about Nikki soon, or I'll go get her back for you!" Ma shouted as I ran down the steps and squealed out of my parents' sex farm as fast as I could.

# ELEVEN

*Nikki*

Over the next week, I went through the motions while working at the taco truck and the strip club. I smudged myself to get rid of any negative energy, but my guilt and sorrow still clung to me like a wet blanket. I did what I had to do for money. And just as Weston had said, he did send my check in the mail. But I didn't have the heart to cash it. I didn't want to cash it. That money had been built on lies and hurt a sweet, old lady and a gentle, big-hearted giant. Only bad things could come from cashing that check.

"What do you mean, you're not cashing it?" Betty cried during food prep. "You mean to tell me, you've been moping around all damn week after that man and his family got you all in your damn emotions, and you don't think you deserve some type of pay from it? Look at you! You ain't Nikki this week! You're a zombie. I can tell something is eating you up, and it's that Jolly Green Giant and his best friend, Dan!"

I looked to Rox for help.

"She's right. Just cash it. Then, do some enchantment or some shit on it. Whatever you have to do. But you said that money would just about pay the rest of your debts off. I think you should do it. If it bothers you, you can find some way to make it up to Weston and his ma. But just cash the damn check and move on." Rox stopped chopping and stared at me, waiting on me to respond.

"You of all people! Like Betty told you, that is your one! Look at you! You're in looooove. You can't even focus! Gosh, that's so cute. Now, you'd better go give him and his ma a grand gesture and make up and live happily ever after!" Layla bounced on her feet, clapping.

"I'm not in love! That shit takes time. And I didn't say I couldn't focus!" I snapped.

"You didn't have to say it. It's written all over your face," Betty sighed.

I touched my face all over as if wiping away my feelings, so the whole world wouldn't know that tough-ass Nikki Vinco from the trailer park felt terrible about doing a little dirty work for money. I never felt bad about stripping. Doing some dirty work for money had always been a part of my life. But the lie I had gone along with for Weston and hurting his ma like I had made me feel like the worst human being imaginable.

"I'll cash it. And then I'll do something nice for the Banks family with it. Weston included. I did have a good time with him." I smiled as I thought about our sneaky sex session in the guest room upstairs.

"Oh, I know you did. I was with an uncut man before, and they are thick! I guess it's all that extra skin!" Layla sucked her bottom lip between her teeth with a smack.

Rox shook her head. "Or maybe he is just that divine intervention you've been looking for. Maybe it has nothing to do with his dick."

"It might have a little bit of something to do with his dick," I said, shrugging my shoulders.

"Of course it did," Betty muttered. "Go get your man. Don't make me drag him back here. Get him and his overbearing ma down here now and explain yourself. The worst-case scenario is, they won't come, or he tells you to fuck off. Then, you'll know you at least tried. And then you can cash that check, guilt-free, job done. But I'll tell you now, Weston is yours. He might not be your usual type, but that's the man you'll end up with and be happier for it. The look in his eyes when he saw you that day back here at the taco truck? He's got it good for you. You'll go far in life with a man like that. Not to mention, the moola." Betty rubbed her fingers together and wiggled her eyebrows.

"Did he really look at me like he liked me?" I asked, grinning. I knew he liked me. I just wanted to reassure myself that everyone else saw what I saw.

*I can't believe that man and his beard have grown on me.*

"Yes!" DTF answered in unison.

"Okay, okay. I'll cash it, call them, set something up, and get this dark cloud of guilt off of me. Crossing my fingers and saying an incantation." I made the sign of the cross, kissed the crystal that hung around my neck, and whispered, "Hallelujah!"

"Praise the Lawd!" Layla shouted, throwing her hands in the air. "The fake Nikki Banks is gonna be banking!"

I twirled a dishrag in the air and slapped her in the butt before getting back to work.

The rest of my workday had been as busy as ever. Crowds gathered around our truck just as quickly as they had left. I tweeted the famous Shizzle Sauce daily specials at lunchtime, and within two hours, we sold out. Our other taco truck that worked the opposite side of town had also sold out during lunch. With business continually picking up, we had a hard time keeping up with the demand. Just this week alone, we'd made an extra nine batches of Shizzle Sauce for Scarlett Herb and fifteen batches for our other taco truck.

By the time I left to volunteer at the cottage, I was too exhausted to do much. Not to mention, my dancing career was tanking because I wasn't able to focus. I missed my bearded giant in the back corner, watching me. Before the fake engagement, he had been a constant fan who I could count on being there even if I had no clue who he was and had thought he was a creeper at first. Now, when I looked out while I was onstage, I only saw dull, dead eyes looking back at me.

The excitement had left my life despite my smudge sticks, despite my crystals, despite my dancing naked under the full moon the other night. I'd had an entire bottle of wine and let loose in the only way I knew how. I'd almost—*almost*—made a booty call to one of my many friends with benefits, but the thought of some halfhearted lay after Weston Banks had screwed me sideways until my eye twitched ... well, that thought had bummed me out. Hence the wine and the drunken, naked moon dancing.

I sat down in front of the teens who had decided to show up today, and I taught them—and myself—how to make beaded jewelry. Two of the young girls were from my old trailer park, and one of them was pregnant. As I explained to everyone the different beads and gemstones and their meanings, they shifted the subject to me and my personal life—a favorite topic of choice with them.

"Who broke your heart?" Trish, the pregnant one, asked.

"Huh? No one. Why would you ask that?" I continued stringing beads on a bracelet I was making for Layla. She hadn't been feeling well lately, and I wanted to give her as much healing vibes as possible.

"Because you are talking monotone, not smiling, and you look like you were punched in the gut." Trish rubbed her belly.

"My boring adult life has nothing to do with jewelry-making," I answered too quickly.

"Who is he?" another teen, Rachel, spoke up.

"Ms. Vinco, tell us, so we can cut him," Trish said, narrowing her eyes and slowly tapping a bead on the desk.

"Why do you kids always want to know about my personal life?" I sighed.

"Because we care. And because you're the only adult who talks to us like an adult and is real with us. Don't you think it's good we learn how the real world is? You were like us once. We want to know how you grew up, how you got where you are today, how you handle things." Rachel sat back in her chair, tossing the bracelet she'd made in front of her.

I rubbed my temples. These kids were smarter than I had been at their age. Maybe the time and efforts I'd put in were beginning to work. I racked my brain on how to turn this into a lesson before letting myself become vulnerable.

"I broke my heart. It was me. I'd made a mistake and hurt some people."

"Ms. Vinco is loving 'em and leaving 'em! I knew it! Didn't I tell you she was one of those player ladies?" Trish bounced in her seat, nodding toward Rachel.

"No. I am not a player lady—because I'm no lady." I winked.

Rachel stuck her knuckles in her mouth. "Damn!"

"Listen, in all seriousness, I did mess up big time. And it's because I lied. I told a big lie and hid myself. In retrospect, I would rather not lie about who I really am, no matter what. I just need to be myself. It took me a very long time to accept myself and my situation and my past. I fell back into the trap of hiding it."

"But why? You hid yourself from this man?" Trish circled her palm along her belly.

"No. Not really. I'm not going to get into specifics. I lied for money. It was a job I took where I had to be someone I wasn't. I would do a lot for money, but that was going too far. I'd never hurt anyone for money, and that is exactly what happened. Learn a lesson, kiddos. Don't lie, accept who you are, try to be the best person you can be, and above all else, don't let some douche bag get you into debt, so you have to work your ass off to climb out of it."

"Happened to my mama too. Her ex stole my and my sister's lunch money in the morning to buy drugs. Not sure what the hell he could get with four dollars, but if he could have a sniff of something to alter his world, he'd gladly pay for it. He's gone now. She's single. Just like me." Trish's voice became low.

"You got this," I said, reaching across the desk to squeeze her hand. "You and that baby are going to be fine. I won't sugarcoat it. Your life will be incredibly tough, but I believe in you. Trish, you're going to be an amazing mom, and that baby of yours might be president one day after she sees how strong her mama is. That will give her the faith to keep going."

The other kids nodded in agreement. I'd never seen a group of children get along and be so supportive of one another in my entire life. They had attached themselves to each other, making their own family in the absence of a family back at their homes.

We sat there for another hour, discussing life, men, debt, and babies. I let the kids carry the conversations and only talked when they asked me a question. Their problems took my mind off my problems, and once again, it showed me perspective.

I reached into my purse and pulled out my phone. I couldn't handle it anymore. I needed to talk to Weston and thank him for the check, double-checking that it was all right to cash it before I went to the bank. I also wanted to hear his voice and see how much damage I'd done to his mom, whom I was sure he had spoken with since. If I could pry her phone number out of him, I'd explain my actions to her. I needed a clear conscience. The smudging had only gotten me so far.

I debated on avoiding an awkward conversation by texting, but I took a deep breath and made my mind up that this conversation was one that needed to be done by voice. I stepped out of the room, scrolled to Weston's name on my phone, and pushed the button to call. He picked up on the second ring.

"Nikki!" Weston was breathing hard, sounding like he had run a marathon.

"Are you okay? It sounds like you're working out or something. Is this a bad time?" I paced the floor in front of the door, fully aware that the girls were probably listening to my conversation.

"No. Not at all. I heard my phone vibrate across the kitchen and had to sprint to get it."

"How big is your kitchen? You sound out of breath."

"It's not very big. I'm lying. I was yanking my crank." He sighed.

"Oh my gosh, Weston! You didn't have to tell me that. Sorry for the interruption!" I leaned against the wall and closed my eyes for a split second, thinking of Weston sitting back in a chair and playing with himself while I rode his face. I quickly shook the thought out of my head.

"You have a sixth sense or something? Did your crystals tell you I was thinking of you just now?"

"You were thinking of me? What was I doing?" My heart plummeted into my stomach, and a warm flush took over my body. I needed to get laid, and no one was doing it for me in my mind, except this giant lump of beard.

"I was thinking of the way your ass had looked when I slammed myself into you, how you'd stared back at me with those bedroom eyes. The expression on your face sent me over the edge. A woman as beautiful as I'd seen in my entire life, looking at me like I was the only thing she wanted. That was what I was just thinking about."

I let out a breath I hadn't realized I was holding and walked toward the end of the hall. "That move you did—hopping to your feet behind me, shoving me forward, and diving in deep and rough—sent me over the edge. I'm a rough fuck girl, and most men are too soft with me. They worry they'll hurt me. But you … surprised the hell out of me. You gave it to me exactly how I wanted. We never really talked about that night, but you are a force to be reckoned with in bed. I had no idea."

"To be honest with you, I've never done anything like that before. I'm still not sure what took over me and made me a wild man. I just wanted you so bad. I had wanted you so bad for a while. And I … I wanted you as mine." His voice trailed off into a sigh.

"Never felt claimed before, but I guess that would be a good word for it. And … I liked it. Kudos to you."

An awkward silence fell over our conversation. I cleared my throat, waiting on him to speak.

"I'm sorry. I can't say that enough. I am truly, truly sorry. And I've learned my lesson. I'll not lie again. I thought I was acting in the best interest of everyone because if I inherited Westworld, I could make it amazing. I know I can. I'm good at that, and I believe in myself enough to do that. I just should have let my parents know that instead of tricking them into what I thought they wanted."

"You thought they wanted? Have you spoken to them? How is Ma?"

"Oh, yes, I have. Ma is okay. More than okay. I need to talk to you about something."

I gritted my teeth. Those last words were always a death sentence. Needing to talk about something was usually a path down a negative road. I braced myself.

"Go on. You can tell me anything." I gripped my crystal necklace in my hand.

"I'd rather talk in person. And it's not just an excuse to see you and apologize to your face again. But that is the icing on the cake—or the cream on your pie, I guess I could say."

"Sounds serious. Are you sure Ma is okay? Did you get written out of everything?" My shoulders slumped as my feet carried me back down the hall and toward the crafts room. My body and mind wanted this conversation to end. Something felt off.

"Everything is fine. Do you dance this week at the club? I can come there and talk, if you don't mind."

"I do. The day after tomorrow. I'll be there at the usual time." I swallowed hard. A serious conversation at the strip club. That should do wonders for my performance.

"Sounds like a plan. Oh, and did you cash your check yet?"

"No. I was going to confirm with you again. I feel like it's dirty money. My conscience would be clearer if I knew everyone was all right and things were good before I cashed it. That's actually why I called. Not because I have some mental voodoo on you jerking off to your fantasy of me."

"If I have to take you to the bank and deposit it myself, you'll clear that check. You worked for it, and everything is okay for you to enjoy it. We are all fine. It's over. Stupid shenanigans."

"Okay. Thanks, Weston. And I'll see you for this serious conversation you're wanting to have soon. Whatever that is all about."

*Is he going to offer me a job?*

*Does he want to date me?*

*Does he want to pay me for something else?*

*Does he want to just be friends and not talk anymore and this is his good-bye?*

*Does he need an opinion on trimming Dan back?*

*It's probably Dan. That would be just like him.*

*Damn it, Weston Banks. This isn't me at all. It's that damn uncut cock!*

"Nothing you'd expect. Trust me. But no worries. I'll see you soon. Get you something nice with that cash too. Don't put it all on a bill. You deserve the best of the best, ex–fake fiancée." He laughed.

"Thanks, ex–fake husband. See you soon."

I hung up the phone and slid it into my back pocket before opening the door to the crafts room. The girls scattered back into their seats.

"Ms. Vinco is a freak! Talking 'bout those jerking-off fantasies!" Rachel laughed.

"I knew it! I knew it!" Trish rocked back and forth in her seat, her gigantic belly jiggling with every laugh.

"Well, you all wanted real talk. Welcome to the real world. Life is full of mess and pleasure. Now, get back to your beads because I need to head out." I gathered my things to go.

"Ms. Vinco, just so you know, you're smiling. Whoever you were talking to done made you do a one-eighty. You have some big, goofy grin on your face like you were the one who just did the jerking off." Trish slipped her bracelet on her wrist and snapped it back.

I reached up, touching my lips as if I needed to confirm with my hand that I was wearing a smile.

"It's a messy life, kids. The truth is, I still haven't figured it out, and you won't either. The best thing you can do is say a prayer and keep going. Never stop. You'll get to where you need to go eventually." I twisted the ring around on my finger and wished I'd had a mother who had told me those words when I was their age.

# TWELVE

*Weston*

Ma slammed the door of the P-wagon shut. "This doesn't look like a strip club. Where are all the neon signs? Why isn't the building painted pink or purple or something? This place just looks like a post office."

"Ma! Stop! I'm having a hard enough time, dragging you in here. It's just weird!" I groaned.

"Son, you've gotta go get the girl. Sometimes, we have to do things we don't want to do. Like bring your parents to a titty bar. Ain't that right, Westy?" Ma laughed.

"Ma! Don't say that word! Gross! I don't know if I can do this. Can we please go back to the Ma who makes cow patties and doesn't swear?" I stopped outside the door of The Steamy Clam.

"When did I swear? And there's a new pile of cow patties on the counter at home! I'm still the same Ma. Just because I had a life before you doesn't mean I'm not the same mom. Now, you just really know more about me as Jean. Don't get your panties in a wad over it. Grow a pair, and let's go," she said, pulling me into the club.

"Better listen to her. If anyone knows how to drop it like it's hot, it's this piece right here," Dad said, slapping Ma's ass.

I bit my tongue, still unsure of this new woman who was my ma but not my ma. I was as confused as ever, but my dad had a new pep in his step. He didn't seem to be affected at all by this sudden change in his wife. I watched them as they giggled like teenagers, hobbling toward the entrance.

*This must be what it means when people say you have to rekindle a marriage. Just remind them who they were before life happened,* I mused, proud of myself for thinking of something Nikki would probably say. I filed that in the back of my mind, eager to share with her how woke I was becoming.

I nodded, giving myself a mental high five, and shuffled my feet through the door.

"Your usual table, Mr. Banks?" The hostess raised her eyebrows and darted her eyes back and forth between Ma and me.

"Yes, thanks." My face flushed hot, but luckily, the club was too damn dark to see anything. I jerked my head to the side, motioning for my parents to follow her.

"Just how many times have you come here? I guess you are your father's son. He showed up at every one of my shows. Stuffed me full of money. I hope you pay Nikki well when she gets up there!" Ma patted my dad on the butt.

"I sure did. Tipped her well. No one could dance like your ma. She could put her back into it." Dad nodded.

I cringed. "I never really paid her. I just watched from the back."

"Weston Banks! I raised a gentleman! What's wrong with you?" Ma said as we all settled into the dark corner table.

"I don't know. I guess I was too shy. She's out of my league."

"Don't ever say that. My son isn't out of anyone's league. You are a catch, and don't you forget it! Nikki is amazing, and so are you. That's why you're going to get her back and wife her up and have them grandbabies of mine."

"She doesn't want kids!" I gritted my teeth.

"I know; I know. I'll never stop suggesting though."

An older waitress came by to take our order.

"Whiskey. Straight. Thanks," I said, wringing my hands under the table before wiping the sweat off of my palms on my blue jeans.

"Sweet tea for us." Ma smiled at the older woman.

"Jean? As in Dragon Lady Jean?" the waitress asked, squinting her eyes.

"Oh, well, I haven't heard that in a long time. Do I know you?" Ma sat upright and peered over her shoulder before returning the gaze of the waitress.

"Peggy. Peggy Pony. We danced together ages ago." The waitress looked at me and winked.

"Oh. My. Lord! Peggy!" Ma said, hopping up and throwing her arms around Peggy.

"I knew it was you! You are still as striking as ever! What brings you here? Westy want to invest in the club? Lord knows, we need it. Our owners are letting this place die out. Girls are quitting left and right. Management is the pits." Peggy shrugged her shoulders and tilted her head toward a corner table full of men in cheap suits.

"I had no idea! That is terrible! No, we are here tonight to support our future daughter-in-law, Nikki."

"She's not your future daughter-in-law, Ma," I said.

"No, not yet she isn't. But my sweet son here is going to marry her one day. I just know it." Ma shook her head, silencing me.

"Are we talking about Nikki as in Crystal Cream Pie?" Peggy asked, shifting her feet.

She looked old enough to be retired, but instead, she was carrying around a heavy waitressing tray and running back and forth on her feet all night. I'd seen her working here before plenty of times. She was my favorite waitress. I'd never known she'd danced with my mother. A shiver ran up my spine, settling into my chattering teeth.

"Yes, Crystal Cream Pie," I said through a clenched jaw.

My dad sat next to me, slapping his knee and laughing. "Wow, just wow. Cream Pie! Kids these days!"

"She's a spitfire, that one. Better watch out. She'll cream your piehole if you get on her bad side. Runs around with the local girl gang, DTF. Amazing group of ladies. Reminds me of us back in our day, Jean. The good old days." Peggy sighed and shook her head. "I'll be right back with your drink order. I think Nikki comes on next."

"Dragon Lady?" I asked as soon as Peggy left the table. "I don't even want to know. I can't believe I'm doing this." I tapped my foot to the rhythm of the woman gyrating onstage as the thought of those big dragon dildos I'd found as a child while meddling in my mother's closet came back into memory. I held back from gagging.

"Would have rather been called something not so mean-sounding, but I had this skit, and it stuck. Do they still do that—skits?" Ma leaned her elbows on the table and watched every move the stripper onstage made.

Dad was entranced as well.

"Watch and see," I said, nodding toward Nikki, who stood at the side of the stage with a cart full of cream pies.

"Oh, we are watching, all right!" My dad leaned forward, clasping his hands together.

Nikki peered around the corner, looking directly at us, her eyes full with a look I'd never seen on her before. Nikki, the badass, was scared.

"Maybe we should have told her we were coming to support her. The poor thing looks like she is about to faint. Here, give me some money, Westy! I'll let her know it's okay." Ma held out her hand while my dad stuffed it full of twenties.

"Here, we'll split it. Let's go down to the stage. You can't let her perform like that. I don't think she's going to make it onstage. Come on." Ma tugged my dad out of his seat and toward the stage.

I followed slowly behind.

The announcer came over the loudspeaker and announced Crystal Cream Pie twice before Nikki snapped out of her trance and pushed her cart to the center of the stage. The audience cheered as my parents and I elbowed our way to the front. Several men stood on the side of the stage, licking their lips and catcalling her. I clenched my money in my fist and put on my game face. I was here to win over this amazing stripper, and I had my parents and my money to back me up. Nikki would be mine again, except for real this time. I hoped.

Nikki looked back and forth from me to my mother to my dad and then back to me.

"Hey there, sexy lady! Show us what ya got!" Ma called, waving a fistful of cash in the air.

Nikki looked to me for an answer, but I only waved my cash in the air, too, and cringed. I had no idea what to say to her. There was no explanation for this awkwardness. All I could do was encourage her to do her own thing. The lights lowered, and the music began. Nikki puffed up her chest, shot me her bedroom eyes, and went to work.

"Good heavens!" my dad said, clutching his chest as Nikki began to strip off her bra.

Gold-glittered pasties covered her nipples, reflecting light off of her chest. She sparkled like a disco ball.

Nikki sauntered over to her pie cart and dipped her finger in the cream before slowly sucking it off. She dipped her finger in it again and grinned, tracing the whipped cream around her chest before taking two whole pies and slamming them into her breasts. The whipped cream dripped down her body, making a mess all around her. She dropped to the floor and slid around in it before walking on her knees over toward a group of men. She pulled one by the back of the hair and shoved his face between her tits, shaking them.

Ma nudged me into the stage. "Get your ass up there, boy, and show her the money! That should be Dan covered in her cream pie!"

I wasn't sure if I was jealous, turned on, embarrassed, or just downright confused. If I could roll myself up into an emotional burrito, that would be my filling—a mixture of *what the fuck.*

Nikki laughed as my ma pointed to me.

"Here! Here!" she shouted.

Nikki grabbed another pie—a fresh one, just for me— and rubbed it all over her chest and stomach. I noticed her take a deep breath before she made her way to the front of the three of us. I couldn't even look at my parents in the eyes, but I did see my dad's palm out of the corner of my eye. He held his money out and pushed it off with his other hand. My dad was making it rain on my ex–fake fiancée.

"For goodness' sake," I cried right as Nikki knelt and shoved my face between her boobs.

My dick twitched in my pants.

*Oh no. I've got to get out of here. This is the weirdest shit ever. Am I horny? Am I humiliated? Am I dying?* I nodded my head to myself on all three accounts.

Nikki leaned over and twitched my ma's nose, making her life. Ma took her twenties and reached over, securely putting them into Nikki's thong and softly patting her butt as if saying, *There, there.*

Nikki shook her head and mouthed, *Thank you,* before returning to the pole and finishing her dance.

She gyrated around the stage in her best performance I'd ever seen. Before her gig was up, the stage was littered with money, and probably half of it was mine.

My dad whistled loud as the music came to a stop. "Son," he said, turning toward me, "that right there is your ma forty years ago. Marry her. She'll make you the happiest man alive."

I nodded, knowing he was right. My life had been turned upside down these past few weeks, but being with Nikki was the only thing that had truly felt right and made sense. We walked back to the table where I dabbed at Dan with a napkin. Ma snatched it out of my hand, wetting it with her spit before smudging it on my face.

"Ma! Gross. Come on now. I got it!" I snatched the napkin back, sitting down into my chair and cleaning myself off.

"So, this is the most awkward family reunion I've ever experienced. Anyone care to tell me what's going on here?" Nikki wore a towel wrapped around her, but she was still covered in cream.

"You were amazing up there!" Ma said, throwing her arms around Nikki. "You know, back in my day, I could make that little move you did there at the end too! When your butt pops up and you do that grind thing! Can't do it now, course, as my hips are bad, but, ah, those were the good old days."

Nikki's eyes grew wide. "I'm sorry, what?" she said, leaning down to hear better over the music that had started back up.

"My mom was a stripper. She met my dad at a strip club. She's finally feeling like her sons are old enough to where she can stop playing mom and be herself. Lucky me. Yay!" I groaned, closing my eyes and trying to make myself disappear.

"Wait a minute. Ma? Were you a stripper? But …" Nikki pulled up a chair and motioned for us all to sit.

"Dragon Lady is what they used to call me." Ma pressed her lips together and nodded. "And no, I didn't do it for money. I did it because I liked it. But when businesses picked up, unfortunately, people didn't like to mix this lifestyle with that one. So, I had to put that part of myself away and focus on career and family. I know it's still like that now, but imagine forty years ago! I lost some good friends when they found out who I was. Thankfully, my parents never knew, but I wished I'd had the type who would support me in my choices. I didn't. So, now, I'm here, supporting my future daughter-in-law. To hell with what people think. Don't put yourself away as I did. You'll only gain resentment."

Nikki's eyes glistened. "This is most definitely not what I expected tonight. I did a terrible thing. I lied to you about who I was. I can't tell you how sorry I am for what I did."

Nikki looked at me, but I quickly shook my head, hoping she understood that I didn't tell them the full story of how we were fake engaged.

"Yes, I'm sorry, too, that we kept her profession a secret from you two. And we made her out to be something she was not," I said, staring at Nikki in hopes that she would understand I was covering for our bigger lie that didn't need to come out.

We'd both learned our lesson on that, so there was no sense in hurting my parents even more.

"I should have been forthcoming with my work. And I shouldn't have told you guys I wanted to be some '50s-style homemaker with a bunch of babies. My kids are at the cottage, where I volunteer, and I am perfectly happy with them. I can't stay home and bake cookies and shit. It's not who I am." Nikki shrugged her shoulders.

"I know it's not. I wouldn't want you to be anything you aren't. That is a long life lesson I learned and the best piece of advice I can give you. Be yourself. Now, on the topic of kids, maybe, one day, you'll change your mind. Maybe not. But you have a good head on your shoulders for my boy here, and nothing is stopping you from becoming one of us. Everything is all right." Ma smiled and patted Nikki's hand.

Nikki's eyes met mine, but I shook my head, still not wanting to spill those beans.

"I look forward to rebuilding the relationship we had, Weston." Nikki scooted her chair closer to mine. "Let's try this again. The right way," she whispered. "If that is what you want."

"All I've ever wanted is you! This whole time. I don't care about your job or if you want kids or not. All I care about is you." I kissed the tip of her nose.

"Thank you all for the support. I'm going to get cleaned up. I'll be back out in a bit. Maybe you can tell me more about this Dragon Lady persona. I'd love to hear all about her," Nikki said, rising from the table.

"She's a fierce one. Just like you, darlin'," Ma called out as Nikki laughed and disappeared back behind the stage.

I had stayed up all night, at a strip club, with my parents and the woman I wanted to not-fake marry, but real marry one day. My mom had told Nikki everything about her past life. I'd never seen her open up like this before, and after watching her light up and talk about the person—or stripper—she used to be, I wasn't uncomfortable anymore. I had gained a newfound respect for my mother.

It wasn't that my childhood had been one big, terrible lie. I realized what my mom had given up to raise my brother and me in the wholesome family lifestyle she created. Not that she didn't like to play that role. She made sure I knew that. She told us she loved every bit of motherhood and still did. But she had lost a part of herself during it all. She had said the sweet but ballsy Crystal Cream Pie had walked into her life and reminded her that she was Jean—Dragon Lady Jean.

She hadn't known why she was so irritable lately. She said she had been exhausted, burned out, annoyed, and even a bit depressed at this stage in life. She had chalked it up to menopause, not the resentment she carried for putting herself away. After her outburst in the kitchen that day of the party, she realized she was tired of playing hostess and staying in the shadows when she had once been in the spotlight. She missed it. Admitting who she had once been and relaxing a bit back into her role as Jean had been a sigh of relief.

*"Here's some dad wisdom for you, Weston. Always support your wife, no matter what. Pay attention to her. I guess I didn't realize all your ma had suppressed. And I'm sorry about that, Jean. I was too selfish, I guess," my dad said, slumping in his seat. "I was so busy with Westworld that I forgot just how feisty and fun you were. Now that the girl I married is back, I'll never let that part of you burn out again! I'm having way too much hot sex for that!"*

*"Westy! Not in front of the kids!" Ma blushed, playfully smacking my father's knee. "And you've always been a supportive partner. Things got busy for both of us. Kids will do that."*

*"It's okay, Dad. That's a valuable lesson you just taught me. I'll make sure that I won't lose sight of my wife or family amid my career. Though I'm not sure this spunky firecracker would ever trade in her stilettos for an apron and Play-Doh," I said, kissing Nikki on the forehead.*

*"Apron? Maybe. Play-Doh? Nope." Nikki shrugged.*

*"It's all right, honey. You've got your hands full with the kids from the cottage. Maybe once things settle …" Ma started.*

*I caught Nikki's eye and winked. I knew she didn't want children, and nothing was going to change her mind from that.*

*"Yes, those cottage kids need me right now. In fact, Weston was asking me about meeting them. You should all come by one weekend and see what we do there. And I'll bring along my girlfriends from the taco truck—DTF." Nikki perked up in her seat.*

*"DTF?" Dad asked.*

*"Dirty. Tough. Female." Nikki smiled. "That's what we call ourselves. They are my best friends and would love to hear about your days as Dragon Lady, Ma. In fact, well, it's not exactly a dragon,*

*but we do have a mascot called Rosie the T. rex, and she's a pretty big deal. We sometimes dress up as her and do different things around town. So, I think you'd all get along really well. Dragon Lady Jean and DTF dinos."*

*"You are already going to be a perfect fit to our family, Nikki," Ma said, laughing and shaking her head.*

*For the slightest moment, I saw the light shine from Nikki's eyes, and that was when I knew she wanted to be a part of us too. Like the fortune teller had told me, for Nikki, our shenanigan hadn't been fake either.*

Since we were too far from home, my parents and I rented hotel rooms for the evening.

I had kissed Nikki good-bye at the club, but I'd whispered in her ear where I was going and that I'd like her to come by. She didn't hesitate in answering with a nod and grin. I had sped off in the P-wagon and chatted about the evening with Ma and Dad until we got to the hotel.

"Man, they need to spruce this place up. New carpet, flooring, add in a business center. Similar to what I'd like to do to our hotel, Dad. And a few other things. I have some ideas for Westworld I want to bounce off of you," I said as we sleepily made our way toward our rooms.

"You're still up for that, aren't you? Taking over, so your old dad can retire and take care of this beautiful lady who needs some attention?" Dad put his arm around Ma and pulled her close.

"You're still okay with letting me do that? Still trust me?" I stopped, pausing in front of their room, and stroked my beard. "Are you sure?"

"Positive. Now, you'll still have to let your brother be second-in-command, but he answers to you. I already talked with him about this, and he took it surprisingly well. Said if things go south, then you get the blame and not him, so he is okay with not being in your shoes and carrying your responsibility. And between you and me, I think he just isn't ready to settle down and grow up."

"No, he isn't. I love him to death, but poor boy will never mature, I'm afraid." Ma hung her head. "He needs perspective. Maybe he'll find someone like you did. I pray for it."

"I'm honored to take over the family business even if it means keeping him on payroll and letting him think he has some say. I think that is the only way to handle him at this point. But thanks, Dad, and thanks, Ma. I won't let you down. Westworld will always be amazing because of the foundation you both built it on."

"Same with you, son. Thanks to your ma, you've been raised on a solid foundation, too, and you're amazing. So, congratulations to the new head honcho." Dad embraced me before turning to unlock his door.

My dad wasn't the most sentimental man I knew, so this level of emotion coming from him had my eyes tearing up and Ma's too.

"Love you, Weston. You're a good man with a big heart. I'm a proud mama. Congratulations. It looks like you've got it all right now. The girl, the career, the family. You deserve it." Ma wiped a tear from her face and threw her arms around me.

"Hear, hear. We can finish this conversation another time. Room's open, Jean. After all that hoopla I saw tonight at the club … I'm feeling in need of a dragon in my bed. I want to make her roar!" Dad smacked Ma's ass and growled.

"Okay, okay. I'm out. That's a bit much. See you two lovebirds!" I said, running to my room, which was thankfully on the other end of the hallway.

I slid the key in the door, shuddered at my parents' last exchange, and texted Nikki my room number before turning on the hot shower. I had told her I would leave the door not entirely shut, but just resting against the lock. She could come in anytime.

I soaped up my johnson and rinsed the sticky remains of Nikki's cream pie off of me. My lips still tasted like whipped cream, and now, I needed them to taste like her. My dick thickened as I closed my eyes and thought about that night back at my parents' house when I had monkey-fucked her from behind. Watching her sweet ass ripple each time I'd slammed into it made my knees shake.

I hurried out of the shower, drying myself off with an oversize hotel towel. I rubbed my cock dry, lingering over the way the soft cotton felt against my bare skin. Earlier today, I had stupidly manscaped my sascrotch, shaving the entire thing off again. You'd think I had learned my lesson after dousing myself in coochie cream, but the thought of bumping uglies with Nikki made me want to be as perfect as possible. She was a goddess. I was a jolly giant. I couldn't measure up, but maybe my dick could.

I walked back into the dark room, throwing the towel onto the floor.

"You're going to just throw that right there instead of putting it up properly?" a voice called from my bed.

I rubbed my eyes, letting them adjust to the dark room. "Nikki?"

"Of course it's me, ya big goober. Who else are you inviting into your bed?" Nikki threw back the covers and slapped the empty side of the bed. "Come on in. Sorry I was a bit late. Stopped to shower and get a few things."

"No, it's fine. You're not late at all. I was talking to my parents for a bit anyway." I slid in next to her.

She was already naked. Her skin prickled the moment I pushed myself against her.

"Everything okay?" Her palm traced slowly down my chest.

"They still want me to take over Westworld." I grabbed her hand and brought it to my lips, kissing it.

"That's awesome! You did it! You got what you wanted!"

She reached over, grasping my face between her hands and smooching me. I gently pushed the back of her head, kissing her harder. Our breaths became heavy, anxious.

She slipped her tongue in between my lips as her hand searched beneath the covers for my dick.

"I don't have all I want. I want you," I growled, crawling on top of her and knocking her knees apart with mine.

"Is that so? I'm in your bed. I'd say, you're off to a good start," she whispered, pushing her hips up to me and rubbing her wet pussy all over my cock.

"No. I want this. I want you as mine. I want to date you. I want you to give me a chance. Not a fake chance, but a real one. Let's see where this goes. I like you … a lot. You talked about divine intervention to me before and how you wanted that in your life. Have you ever thought that maybe you're divine intervention to someone else? Maybe that is your role to play. You're the special person who unexpectedly shows up and turns someone else's world upside down for the better."

She grabbed Dan and pulled him toward her face so that our eyes were only inches apart. "Weston Banks, that is the damn sexiest thing anyone has ever said to me in my life. I guess I can give you that chance." She grinned.

"You guess?" I tilted my head, kissing her forehead, her cheek, her nose, and working my way down.

"Did I say that?" she breathed out, moaning and bucking her hips.

I trailed my lips over her body until I reached the soft flesh between her legs. I slid my tongue down her slit.

"What I meant to say was, hell yes. Weston Banks. Hell. Yes!" she cried out as I lubed up my beard with her juices.

I let her squirm under my mouth before I crawled my way back up her body. She pulled a condom from beneath the pillow beside her.

"Another reason I had to stop at the house. I know your ma wants grandbabies, but I sure as shit don't," she said, tossing the rubber at me.

I tore it open with my teeth and rolled it on.

"I won't give you those if you don't want them. But I do want to give you everything," I whispered, leaning over her and sliding myself into home.

She wrapped her legs around my waist and pulled me in tight with her ridiculously strong thighs.

"You already have," she moaned, her breath tickling softly against my neck.

And then I made Nikki Vinco mine.

# EPILOGUE

*Nikki*

I lazily tapped my pen against the notepad on my lap. The sun shone down into my backyard, reflecting bright light off the white paper.

"Who would have thought, Nikki Vinco, trophy wife?" Betty loudly slurped her daiquiri through a straw.

"Nope, nope, nope. Nikki Vinco … Nikki Vinco …" I struggled to define what I had become seemingly overnight.

Just a short month ago, I had been a stripper, and now, I had eloped and become a married woman.

"Oh. My. Gosh. I'm Nikki Banks now! I am a fucking trophy wife. Shit!" I chewed my bottom lip.

I'd never expected to get married, especially not into the Banks family. But after a dream in which my mom had come to me and told me to say yes, I said yes to everything that came my way over the next few days. I didn't know if she was telling me to tell the barista, *Yes, I want whipped cream*, or tell the girls, *Yes, I can work an extra shift*, or tell

Weston, *Yes, I will elope with you.* So, I had answered yes to it all—including Weston's proposal.

He had taken me to the farm one weekend for a relaxing getaway. His parents were gone on their second honeymoon, rekindling their newfound sexual awakening, according to Ma. She had told Weston we could stay at their place for the weekend, except for no nooky before the wedding. She was still adamant about it being bad luck, and she said we didn't need any of that in the family. There were still parts of Ma left. She wasn't only Dragon Lady Jean these days.

We snuck in a bottle of champagne, and Weston packed us a picnic lunch. He drove us back down to the mud pit, where we dined, drank, and ran around the creek but naked. I had no idea why we were naked, but it was fun, and it felt good to immerse myself in Mother Earth. Everything had felt safe, right, comfortable.

*"You aren't afraid of pee fish anymore?" I asked as we waded our naked bodies into the creek.*

*"Turns out, those fish aren't from around here. I Googled." He put his arms around my waist and pulled me into him.*

*"Is that right?" I smirked. "You came prepared then." I ran my palm along his cheek, letting it trail down his beard. A hard lump stuck out of Dan. "What the hell? Is Dan growing his own beard? A tumor? What the fuck?"*

*"Well, it wasn't supposed to go down this way, but we got naked, and I panicked. I didn't know where else to stick it. My only other option was most definitely not an option. Here." Weston pulled out a tiny box from his beard and swallowed hard, handing it to me.*

*"Is this jewelry? Did you stash jewelry in your beard?" I laughed, prying open the tiny velvet box. Inside was the ring I had worn for our fake engagement.*

*"It's real this time. And I know this is all happening quick. But I love you and I'm sure about this and I want you. I know you were meant for me. I hope you believe I was meant for you too. Will*

*you marry me, Nikki?" Weston's chest rose and fell dramatically. The poor man looked on the verge of nervous tears.*

*I hesitated, checking in with my brain, my soul, my heart. I remembered my dream and my mother urging me to say yes. If that wasn't a sign, then what happened next was.*

*Bessie trampled down to the creek, interrupting us with her incessant mooing. She stomped around in the water, tossing her head back and forth.*

*My jaw dropped. I'd never seen a damn cow act like this before. I wondered if she had eaten some mushrooms or something. "What's she say about it?" I asked Weston.*

*"She told me that you'd better say yes, or she will stampede your ass." Weston's jaw dropped. "Bessie! That is just rude!"*

*"And this is just weird. But I guess there's your answer. I don't want to get rammed by that heifer. The answer is yes," I said, slipping the ring over my finger.*

*Oddly enough, Bessie gave one last moo and left us alone.*

*"Can't believe I'm marrying a cow whisperer." I laughed. "Can't believe I'm even getting married, to be honest."*

*"Me either! The stars must be aligned!" Weston cried out, swooping me up in his arms and kissing me hard on the lips.*

We had married at the courthouse two days later, much to Ma's dismay. She made us promise to have a real wedding on the original date we had planned, her wedding anniversary next year. We had gone along with it, hoping her idea would fizzle out. But if I had to choose between a wedding or babies to please Ma, I would choose the wedding.

"And you are loving every moment of being a trophy wife!" Layla chimed in, interrupting my daydreaming. "Seriously, why can't I find a rich, giant lump of hair like Weston?"

"Wear some crystals, dance in some platforms, howl at the moon. Have you tried that, Layla?" Rox shielded her eyes from the sun.

We'd been spending the entire afternoon lounging by the pool and working on my business plan. Weston's wedding gift to me was a 501(c)(3). He said that Westworld would build Outer Forks a top-notch youth center for all ages and all incomes. He had the bright idea that if every child was welcome, maybe the more advantaged children could befriend the less advantaged children, and everyone could learn different perspectives and be woke. Yes, Weston said *woke*. He wanted to build the big home on ten acres with a bunch of kids running around, as he had predicted in his future, except the children weren't exactly his and the house was the youth center. He was as excited about it as I was—maybe even more so. I didn't think I could be more proud of my hairy husband.

"I don't think it's the crystals. I think it's the boobs and her cream pie." Betty hiccuped.

"Everyone loves a cream pie," Rox said.

"But seriously though, Nikki, how does it feel to have all of this? Look around. You made it, lady. You were in debt, living in a tiny apartment, dating losers. Now, you have a mansion, an amazing family, and you don't have to strip anymore—or work at all. You are an inspiration!" Layla said.

"I'll never quit the taco truck. That's my girl time. But I might have to put in fewer hours once this nonprofit gets off the ground, which brings me back to it. Help me out, y'all. What should I call it? Outer Forks Youth Center is too boring."

"Your mother's name?" Rox and the rest of DTF looked at me, unsure of how I would react.

I rarely talked about my mother. She'd left a hole inside of me that I wouldn't ever be able to fill. But she had been troubled, and I understood that now. She'd deserved the best, and even though she had been absent for much of my life, I knew she had tried. It was her poor choices that had fucked my childhood up. I'd followed in her footsteps with the bad decisions, too, until I found support in my girl gang. DTF had shown me that I was worth more.

"You could name it after both your mom and Weston's mom since you now have two mothers." Betty nudged me with her elbow, smiling.

"Are you being sentimental? You? Betty? Wow! How much have you had to drink?" I took a long-drawn-out sip of my daiquiri.

"Enough to say, I told you so. I told you Weston was your man. That Jolly Green Giant done hooked you up, and now, you can live your dream while helping everyone else live theirs." Betty set her cup down on the table beside her and leaned back in her lounge chair.

"Does that mean you'll finally let me put an enchantment on Terrance?" I asked, twisting the wedding ring on my finger.

"Don't need an enchantment for a man when you have these boobs!" Betty lifted her breasts and then let them fall in her famous boob drop.

"What was your mother's name anyway? I don't think you've ever told us," Rox asked.

"Crystal," I sighed.

"Are you serious? Crystal? As in Crystal Cream Pie and all those crystals you got lying around and ... well, shit! It all makes sense now!" Betty sat back up, rubbing her chin. "Crystal Jean's Center for Youth. Is that better?"

"Yes. I think you just named our youth center, Betty." I smiled, jotting it down in my notepad.

"Drunk Betty is deep." Betty hiccuped, farted, and groaned.

"And that's why you haven't landed Terrance," Layla said in a singsong voice.

"I think it's more because Terrance hasn't landed her." Rox laughed.

"Bingo!" Betty made air guns with her hands, pretending to shoot the sky. "Pow! Pow!"

DTF burst into laughter.

"Whoa, whoa, whoa! What's all this racket out here?" Ma said, coming through the back patio to join us. She carried a tray of fresh cow patties in her hands.

"Mama Jean!" Layla said, clapping her hands. "Come and sit next to me! Nikki has some news to tell you!" Layla patted the side of her lounge chair.

"You're pregnant!" Ma cried, almost toppling over her plate of cookies.

"No! You know my kids are at the center. We are never going to stop having this conversation, are we?" I asked, reaching across and grabbing a cookie from her plate.

"Nope. You girls are getting ripe. All of y'all need to start popping out babies before it's too late. I'm telling you, kids are amazing. Life-changing," Ma said, munching away on one of her cookies.

Betty snored loudly from a few lounge chairs down.

"Drunk Betty," I sighed. "She is the person who gave us this brilliant idea I'm about to share with you. I was looking for a name for the youth center, and I want to name it after my mother … and you. So … both of my moms. Crystal Jean's Center for Youth. Are you okay with that?" I asked between bites of cow pattie.

Ma burst into tears. "Who needs grandbabies when I have a daughter-in-law like you?"

"So, I'm off the hook for grandbabies?" I raised my eyebrows.

"I'm not that easy," Ma muttered. "But you're rubbing off on me a little. Maybe I can help you out at the center. Maybe you can have some type of daycare in the place, and I can get my baby fix. In the meantime, Westy purchased The Steamy Clam since Peggy Pony said it wasn't doing too well. We want to help them girls and give them all living wages and even start a college program for them."

"Now, there is a brilliant idea! Those girls are going to be so happy to have you as a supporter, Ma! I'd love to help in that area too! As for the daycare, that will work for sure. I bet Rox knows some moms from the shelter she volunteers at who need jobs and childcare. It's all coming together now!" I took another sip of my drink and scribbled down more notes.

Weston ran out of the patio door and cannonballed into the pool, nearly missing us with his whale-sized splash. His beard hung off his chin in a soaking wet mess, much like how I had seen it last night when we fooled around in bed. I'd never known a beard ride could feel so damn good, but Weston's chin 'fro tickled me in all the right ways.

"Did someone call for a pool boy?" he asked, slowly pulling himself up the ledge of the pool.

Betty laughed in her sleep—or at least, her pretended sleep—and my new husband wasn't making an oddball fool of himself. I'd been working on his wardrobe to bring him a little bit more up to my standards, but I kept his quirkiness factor. I loved the P-wagon, I loved Dan, I loved how he called me a geode, and I loved him. At least I thought I did. I had never been in love before, but if I were to fall in love, it would feel like this and with someone like my husband and his family. My family.

I felt the tingles from my drink buzz up into my brain, making me light-headed and fuzzy. "Come on over here, pool boy!" I winked.

Ma told Weston about our plans and DTF. All, except Betty, joined in on the conversation, throwing out ideas left and right. I quietly sat back and ran my index finger over the ring my mother had given me long ago. I had always wanted a family—a mom and a dad, brothers, and sisters. And now, I didn't have that conventional family, and I likely never would, but my friends and my new husband and parents were my family now, and I couldn't be happier.

"Sometimes, you have to embrace the life you've got and release the one you thought was for you. Funny how what we think we want usually comes to us in a totally different package. But as long as you're still getting those needs met, who cares how it comes as long as it comes?" Rox said, leaning over to squeeze my hand.

"Divine intervention?" I asked, smiling back at Rox.

"No, honey. This is the result of the efforts you put in. Someone is looking out for you, for sure, but this"—Rox motioned around my new home and backyard with her hands—"you earned it. And that too." She nodded at Weston, who remained in deep conversation with his mom and Layla. "That man right there loves you more than anything in this world and will always take care of you. You earned him too."

"But I don't want a man to take care of me. I want to take care of myself. You know that." I pursed my lips, tapping the pencil on the side of my notebook.

"You do, and you will. You have the drive and the focus. But sometimes, it's okay to let someone else take the wheel too. Anyone in your family will drive for you when you need us to. And I mean that. DTF and Banks. I love you, and I'm proud of you. Crystal would have been too." Rox kept her voice low, trying to have a private conversation amid Betty's snores and Layla's guffaws.

"Thanks, Rox. DTF is going places. We all are. I can feel it." I scooted closer to her, leaning over to hug her.

"That's why we support our local girl gangs," Rox whispered into my ear.

"DTF!" cried a drunken Betty from her sleep, interrupting our conversation.

"DTF!" everyone answered back, including Ma, our newest member.

I laughed as I looked around at my new family and sent up a quick thank-you prayer to whoever would listen. I let whoever was looking out for me up there know that I would pass on the love, the knowledge, the light. Sometimes, a divine intervention could come in the form of a stripper from the local trailer park.

# THE END

WANT MORE DTF?
READ ON FOR THE FIRST CHAPTER
FROM *WHIP IT OUT*.

# WHIP IT OUT

## ONE

*Betty*

"This used to be my safe nest, and now, look at it." Rox shook her head. Her hands curled around an iron bar as she popped it into place.

"Yeah, it's still a safe nest. If you know the safe word." I held the other end of the bar and fumbled with the directions in my hand.

We had been putting my sex swing together for three hours, and we still couldn't get it right.

"Did you order this thing used or something? Is it missing parts? Can't we just call Jay?" She groaned, raking her fingers through a pile of screws and bolts.

"Damn it, Rox. We don't need a man. We're going to set up my playroom like the badass bitches we are. DTF. Dirty. Tough. Female. Has Jay got you forgetting who you are? We can do this. Now, hand me that long metal thing beside you."

"That's an Allen wrench, Miss Independent." Rox tossed the tool next to me and smiled. "He does have me goo-goo-eyed still, doesn't he?" She let out a long-drawn-out sigh.

"Keep that mess to yourself. You see, y'all have something special. But me? If I were to find a man like that, no good would come of it, I'm telling ya. All the women in my family have been divorced. Some more than once. You know that. It just doesn't work out for us Willis women like that. If I fell in love with a man like your Aussie next door, he would have a secret family still over there in the Down Under. I'd only find out about her and his babies after he died." I stuck the Allen wrench in a hole, as per the instructions, and began to tighten the legs on my new toy.

"Bullshit. You know your conniving ass would find out way before he died. That's why you got this room, isn't it? You tie these poor men up and make them tell you everything, so you can protect yourself when you move forward with them."

I set the wrench down and blinked. "Huh. I never thought about that. I always just thought I liked to dominate their asses. But that was some deep stuff you said. I take it, you're still in therapy."

"You know it."

"Proud of you. Even if you're peeling the layers of me back and exposing some shit I don't want to think about. So, cut it out. Let's just pretend that whip over there is for pleasure and not protection." I tilted my chin in the direction of a rack that held not one, or two, or three leather whips, but eight.

I had a whip of every size for a man of every size.

Tall and lanky?

Check!

Short and muscular?

Check!

Dad bod incoming?

Check!

I wasn't picky, but lately, I'd been leaning toward the stereotypical ripped-up men. Blame it on all of the male strippers I'd been eyeing lately at The Steamy Clam. Thanks to our ever-so-popular stripper friend Nikki, better known as Crystal Cream Pie, my taste in men had changed slightly. I never knew what a pair of pecs could do for me until I saw Terrance shake it onstage. Even after Nikki quit dancing, the girls and I would still stop by the club and have a good time.

"Let me get this straight. What you're saying is, we're putting up this sex swing, so you can finally invite Terrance over and torture him until he tells you all his secrets. Then, you can let yourself fall in love with him." Rox rose to her feet and snapped another iron bar into place.

A chill ran up my spine. Ever since Rox and Nikki had been messing with all those crystals and otherworldly stuff, I swore, sometimes, I thought they could read my mind, just like right now. I'd been thinking of Terrance, and Rox had sensed it.

"Can you get out of my head, please? Why don't you open up shop as a fortune-teller? You and Nikki. Take Layla too. I'll run The Pink Taco Truck, and y'all three can use your crystals and voodoo to fight crime or some shit. Get people laid. Go out into the world and do what you got to do to make it a better place." I pushed myself off the floor and reached for the other side of the swing, picking it up and joining it with the other half.

"I'm just saying, you've been eyeballing him for months. Y'all always flirt at Scarlett Herb when he's making your drinks. And then, when he dances, you're his number one fan. So, why haven't either of you asked the other out yet? Or at least fucked. One-night stand? Hello? What's wrong with you? The man is hot!" She pushed down hard on the roped seat of the swing, checking its sturdiness.

"You heard what Jay told us when we first started hanging around his bar. He said that Terrance has women in and out of there all the time. Some old ones, some young ones. He's into a little bit of everything. So, to me, it sounds like Terrance—aka stripper Tito—is a playboy. Why else would he be stripping? I'm sure he makes enough off all the tips he's pulling in. I know Jay pays his workers living wages. I'm not getting involved with Terrance or Tito or anyone who's going to put me on a list. One-night stand? Maybe. But I don't need all that right now. I'm working, paying bills, slaying goals." I sat my ass down in the swing and pushed through my heels, sending my body flying backward and my legs up to the ceiling.

"Good Lord. Is that what you're going to do in that thing? I might need to borrow it. Who's going to be the first to test it out anyway? If you say you aren't getting involved with a man, then what's all this for?" She motioned around my sex dungeon.

"I didn't say I don't have sex. I have friends with benefits. You know, the usual gang. I don't know yet who's going to get into this thing. Mike, Larry, Kenneth—"

"Tito."

"Girl, please. No time for a playboy."

"I see. So, only you're allowed to be the playboy in the relationship." She rubbed her chin. "You should still ask him out. Maybe he isn't a playboy. Or maybe he is, but he might change if he met the right person."

"Now, I know your ass needs to go back to therapy. You can't change a person!" I skidded to a stop.

"I'm not saying you can! I know you can't, believe me. You know I know that. But I'm saying if he saw something he wanted—like your tall, fine black ass dressed in leather and holding a whip—then maybe, just maybe, he would cut all that riffraff out and be yours. I mean, most people stop looking once they meet the right one. It's not you changing anyone. It's just them not caring about anyone else once they see perfection." She walked over to the bed and let herself fall back on my new, bouncy mattress.

I detangled myself from the straps of my swing and followed her to the bed, plopping myself on my back beside her.

"I'm not anything close to perfection. No one is." I rubbed my palms over my tired eyes.

"No, we aren't perfect. But … you're wrong in saying you're not close. You're close to perfection for the right person."

"There you go with that la-la love-land shit you're in."

She propped herself up on her elbow, staring down into my face. "What is it you want then? You're thirty-one. Don't you want kids and a family? I know you do, Betty. Don't play tough with me."

"I have my nieces for family. What I want is, not to lose focus on my work and fall into poverty. I grew up that way, you know. Have you ever felt hunger, Rox? Do you know how many days I'd sometimes go without a meal? Ever gone to school for days on an empty stomach? I'd sneak to the back of the line, so I could pick food off trays when everyone set them on the counter to be thrown out. What if something happened and I couldn't provide for my children?"

"What in the hell are you talking about? You work with me. We own two taco trucks. We're both financially stable and independent. I know you are if I am. I know how much you make. We're a team. You just moved into my old house! Are you on crack? You've got it all. If you ever say you're going to wait until you're ready, you'll never get what you want. And I know you. Play tough all you want, but I know you. There's a heart somewhere in that cold, dead soul of yours. I know it because I hide mine too. That's why we're best friends."

"I thought we were best friends because we knew too much about each other." I rose on my elbow to meet her gaze.

"That too." She laughed.

"I do have it all." I glanced around my room.

Just a few short months ago, I had lived in an apartment that was crumbling before my eyes. Literally. When I banged my ex-boyfriend in there, anytime my headboard hit against the wall, dust would fall in our eyes from the old, retro ceiling. To make matters worse, it was one of those glittery ceilings. When we finished screwing, we'd both look like we'd stepped out of a dirty disco.

"Just not a man."

"Yep. And who says we need a man? Look at that. We just put that together all by ourselves." I nodded toward the swing, which made a squeaking noise, shifted, and collapsed on the ground.

"I rest my case," Rox muttered, hurling herself off the bed and walking toward her phone that she had placed on the dresser. "I'm calling Jay, and he'll bring some power tools. Then, we're finishing your sex dungeon within the next hour or two. While he's here, grill him about Terrance. Or I will. I see the way he looks at you and the way you look at him. Wouldn't hurt to try it out. Besides, what do you have to lose? You said it yourself. You have it all."

I bit my tongue. I couldn't argue with her on that. For once, I was happy and settled in life. If I added a man into the mix, that could all change. Given my family's track record on relationships, my entire life could be turned upside down by one douche bag. I rolled my eyes into the back of my head and lay down again.

"Fine. Call Jay. Let's get this damn thing together. But I'll be the one asking the Terrance questions."

"Good. And anything you don't find out, you can bring him over here and whip it out of him. Make that playboy pay for his naughty behavior! Show him who's boss!" She thrust her hips in the air and made a spanking motion with her palm before turning her attention to her phone.

I closed my eyes, drowning out the sounds of her conversation with her boyfriend, and focused on the next steps in my life. I'd not given any thought to it before. I'd learned from my childhood to live one day at a time. The only planning for the future I'd ever done was financial. But now, I was settled, and now, I had no idea what came next. I didn't need anything to come next, but I wasn't getting any younger. The thought of kids and family terrified me, but that tiny heart Rox had mentioned did ache for that so-called American dream one day. That day just wasn't going to be today or tomorrow or the next few years. I'd been saving every cent, and both kids and men could wipe out my cash quicker than I'd saved it—which had taken me years.

*Nope, I'm not yet ready,* I thought to myself. *I've got too much work to do, too much planning, saving for …*

I had no idea what I was saving for.

*My future kids' college funds one day? Big house on ten acres? A vacation home in Greece?*

"He'll be right over," Rox said, interrupting my thoughts.

It was a welcome interruption. These deep thoughts needed to go.

"You got one of the good ones, you know. You're lucky." I smiled, genuinely proud of my friend. I hadn't seen her this happy ever.

When Jay had walked into her life, Rox shone brighter than any of the DTF crew could imagine. I didn't want to get all crazy like Nikki and believe the hocus-pocus, but Jay and Rox were proof enough of how someone could walk into your life and change the course of your path forever.

"Thanks. I know. It's an amazing feeling. We're going to get your dark soul to feel it. You think you're doing good and have it all now? Wait until you meet *the one.*" She sighed, letting herself free fall again onto my bed.

"Uh-huh. The one had better not fuck up what I have. I've worked too hard for it. I'm happy. Whoever he is, he'd better be perfect."

"Not perfect, but damn near it. I promise he will be. You just need to slow down on working all the time and open your eyes. It's time. You deserve it." She rolled over and kissed the top of my forehead. "Just don't show him this room until much, much later into your relationship. I think those things might scare some men off." She nodded toward a shelf where dildos of all shapes and sizes were displayed.

"He's gonna like me for me. And this is me."

"True that," she agreed. "Just hide that spiked one at least. And maybe the dragon one you got from Weston's ma. Take it out once you've got him bound to this bed and talking but not before."

"Girl, I got this." I huffed on my nails and polished them against my chest.

# PLAYLIST

Do you want to keep rocking out with Nikki and Weston? Check out a sample of the official *Cream-Pied* soundtrack below. For the full playlist, visit Spotify and search for Kat Addams and keep on rocking.

"Darling Nikki" | Prince

"Who Are You" | The Who

"Low Rider" | War

"Bad Reputation" | Joan Jett & The Blackhearts

"Wild Side" | Mötley Crüe

"More Than a Feeling" | Boston

"Livin' on a Prayer" | Bon Jovi

"Marry Me" | Train

# ACKNOWLEDGMENTS

To my daughter—I hope you have the confidence, growing up, to stay true to yourself and be who you are meant to be. I will always support you in life, no matter what. You are going to go far, kiddo. I'll make sure of it.

Thank you to my editor, Jovana Shirley, and my cover designer, Lori Jackson. I couldn't do any of this without you two. My books would look like something out of a middle school grammar assignment and PaintShop Pro if I didn't work with the both of you. Thank you, thank you for your hard work!

Thank you to the bookstagrammers out there for working hard to share all of my crazy stories. I appreciate all of you! You truly make our jobs as authors more exciting. I am so glad to have become friends with many of you! Thank you for all of your hard work.

Thank you to the mamas who've had to give up a piece of themselves to raise children in the best way they know how. I see you, and you're doing an amazing job.

And lastly, thank you to the supporting roles out there, helping those who need it. The volunteers, the friends offering an ear to listen, the family members helping to pick up pieces, the cycle-breakers, and the world-changers. Thank you for making this planet a better place.

# ABOUT THE AUTHOR

Kat Addams is a forever twenty-nine-year-old fashionista following her lifelong dream of writing contemporary romance inspired by the exotic men she meets in her worldly travels. At least, that's what she would like for you to think. She's certainly not a stay-at-home mom indulging in excessive daydreaming, frozen pizzas, an unhealthy addiction to purchasing pajamas, and one too many cocktails on the regular. That's some other romance author. The poor thing probably has to sneak away upstairs to write her dirty stories! What would her family think? Thankfully, that's not Kat!

Social Media:

Still crazy about Kat? Rawr! Stalk her on the social media platforms linked below!

https://linktr.ee/author_kat_addams

(For all of the links in one convenient location!)

Newsletter: https://kataddams.com/free-book

(Bonus *Hotty Toddy* Free E-Book)

Want to keep up with all the mischief and bad decisions? Be sure to subscribe to Kat's newsletter for the latest news. By becoming a subscriber, you'll be the first to know the juicy details on upcoming releases, special offers, exclusive content, sneak peeks, terrible ideas, ridiculous shenanigans, and more! As a special gift for signing up, you'll also receive a free e-book, *Hotty Toddy.*

Goodreads:
www.goodreads.com/author/show/
19253462.Kat_Addams

Bookbub:
www.bookbub.com/profile/kat-addams

Amazon:
http://amazon.com/author/kataddams

DTF, Dirty. Tough. Females. (A Kat Addams Reader Group): https://www.facebook.com/groups/DirtyToughFemales/

(A Facebook group to stay connected, laugh, and share. Hope to see you there!)

Facebook: www.facebook.com/KatAddamsAuthor

Instagram: www.instagram.com/authorkataddams

Twitter: https://twitter.com/KatAddamsAuthor

ARC Team: https://docs.google.com/forms/u/2/d/e/1FAIpQLScinoImFEIChW3PQ4_BrlBoYxpcClYTftNZRz-1DmI-121R8A/viewform?usp=send_form

(Join the team if you're interested in receiving Kat Addams's latest books before release.)

# OTHER BOOKS BY KAT ADDAMS

## DIRTY SOUTH SERIES

*Hotty Toddy (Free for newsletter subscribers:*
*https://kataddams.com/free-book)*

*Grit and Grind*

*Nashvegas Nights*

*Mr. Big Ego*

*Mayday*

## DTF (DIRTY. TOUGH. FEMALE.) SERIES

*On the Rox*

*Cream-Pied*

*Whip it Out*

*Just the Tip*